Fighting off a sudden chill, Katherin⟨e⟩ Through the swirling flakes of snow slowly down the path between the lake ⟨and⟩ man dressed in a long dark overcoat and a black knit hat.

Katherine put her coffee down, quickly butted her cigarette in an ashtray and moved toward one end of the sliders. She cocked her head in an attempt to see the modest parking area between her house and the next cottage, but it revealed only her old Ford Bronco. It was virtually unheard of to see a stranger this time of year, particularly on foot.

The man was at the base of the steps now.

He glanced in both directions then lifted a pair of black eyes to the sliders, his lips pursed, trails of mist tumbling from his nostrils as his breath hit the frigid air.

As she held his dead stare, Katherine felt another chill trickle across her spine. She did her best to appear unaffected. "Can I help you?" she asked, raising her voice so it could be heard through the glass.

The man stared at her but offered no response…

A VIEW
FROM THE LAKE

BY GREG F. GIFUNE

DEDICATION

For Boomer, with the same boundless love she always showed me.

ACKNOWLEDGMENTS

I am honored to have TM Wright's kind and thoughtful introduction as a continued part of this book. Terry was a true master, and he led the way for many of us with his brilliant and groundbreaking work. Terry was not only one of my mentors, he was a friend. Sadly, we lost him in 2015. I will always be grateful not only for his contributions to our business and our art, but for his friendship and kindness as well. Also, thank you to David Wilson for believing in my work, and for getting this novel back in print. And as always, thanks to my wife Carol, my family and friends, and a special thank you to my readers and fans across the globe for their continued support.

INTRODUCTION

BY T M WRIGHT

Life and death, and all the flotsam and jetsam swirling around and between, are mysteries. And, in my opinion, good writers don't try to solve those mysteries; they simply write about them, sometimes stunningly well.

Greg F. Gifune is a good writer.

Think about this a moment: is it possible that *death*, in all its repellant, hypnotic glory, may simply be a state of mind? Could it be only what we *believe* it to be, or, more likely, could it be a matter of one plain of existence—*life*—being set aside, consciously or not, for another—*death* (if we can accept death as a "plain of existence", and, hell, why not?). But wouldn't *life*, then, have to be just a state of mind, too, which would mean that if death and life are interconnected, then we, as intelligent, passionate beings capable of dreaming large dreams, nightmarish and otherwise, and capable, too, of existential decisions, would be able to redefine what "death" and "life" and the small, or incredibly large, universe their intermingling creates, amounts to, or can amount to, perhaps a new plain of existence that may or may not be connected to the (pardon this word) *continuum* that the merging of *life* and *death* creates.

Greg F. Gifune is an exquisitely talented writer, and *A View from the Lake* (read and translate that title carefully) is an exquisitely written, often quietly creepy and terrifying novel, not only because, in it, Mr. Gifune shows us he knows well that good fiction can also sometimes be a form of grim poetry that grips our imaginations, but because, in *A View from the Lake*, he has a story to tell, a mystery to unfold, about life and death and the dark passions and hellish secrets that attend both, and his impressive strengths as a storyteller are very much in evidence.

A blizzard is one of the non-sentient characters in *A View from the Lake*. Throughout the novel, it grows slowly, from an almost graceful, almost beautiful threat to, at last, a shrieking demon of chaos. That's important—a blizzard as a form of chaos. Because death itself, as we have come to view it, signals the very *end* of chaos. But chaos, for us, the living, can erupt when the sudden, or even not-so-sudden loss of a loved one overwhelms us and makes us believe that the universe we've come to think of as unchanging, dependable, and even benign, is, all at once, something we don't recognize, something that may mean us harm. And we may come to realize that what we've grown to think of as "our" universe (our home, our street, the people who love us and whom we love back) our *island*, free of incursion by forces we can't predict, is simply a fantasy which can last only for a very brief part of a life, until the larger universe, the *real* universe beyond the one we've built for ourselves, shows us that our fantasies mean nothing at all. And that's when chaos erupts; when we don't know what the great universe that exists from deep within us to far, far beyond—is going to do to us.

Chaos can erupt, as well, when a loved one leaves us—through death or otherwise—and although, in any of several ways, the loved one has signaled he still exists, we can not find him, try as we might. And we try very, very hard.

What's in a name? Blissful Point, a resort for lovers and others—anyone looking for contentment, anyone looking for…bliss. But bliss is no longer available and it's time to close the resort, time to live alone. And keep looking.

And what about "insanity", portrayed in this novel as a loss of connection with reality, as *inner* chaos, which takes over by slower, not as graceful, ultimately not as noisy degrees as the physical chaos of a blizzard, but which, at last, has more profound effects.

And when one who is loved is taken from us, by death or insanity, or otherwise, we suddenly need that loved one more than we may have ever needed him; and it's a need which can last for years, a need which we may, by turns (and possibly at the same time), embrace and reject; but it's a need which can not be ignored. Unlike the blizzard, we are sentient beings.

Like all good writers, Greg Gifune knows about people, knows what pulls them from day to day, knows how they react—in the various and sometimes disparate ways people react—to fear and anger, love and regret, need and hunger and passion. And you'll find that the people who populate A View from the Lake (Katherine and her poet husband, James, and her friend Carlo, plus several vitally important *others*) are not simply as real as the people you deal with every day, they will also surprise you, though, here, in very different ways than the people you deal with every day surprise you.

Ask yourself this: How well do I know the one I love? The one who professes to love me. Do I know him or her beyond all the quirky habits, predilections, tastes, humor, et cetera that our loved one presents to us (as his "real self")? Do I know his secrets? Hell, do I know the secrets he keeps from *himself*? And if I know those "secrets", do I know *all* of them? In other words, do I really *know* the one I love, the one who professes to love me, as well as, or even better than, I know myself? Do I know him beyond the fact that he feeds his cooked carrots to the dog while I'm not looking? Do I know him beyond the fact that he's had three times as many lovers as he's admitted to? Do I know him beyond knowing what he does behind locked doors?

I think we all realize that our loved ones harbor secrets; perhaps many, and that these secrets are, indeed, "secrets" because our loved ones don't want to share them—perhaps even with themselves.

In A View from the Lake, Katherine comes to realize that the secrets lovers keep from one another can go much deeper, and can be much more sinister, than secrets involving what gets fed to the dog when we're not looking. Sometimes those secrets, if revealed, can create a blizzard of chaos in which not a snowflake falls.

I love cats. They're beautiful, deadly, and almost preternaturally silent when they need to be. They're also incredibly patient. They can stare at one spot, nearly without sound or motion, for hours. My wife Roxane and I have three cats—Nilsson, Dylan, and Weldon; all named after poet/writers, because cats are graceful, lyrical, and, in ways that only cats can be, spiritual.

I like to think that ghosts are similar to cats (and A View from the Lake features a cat named Barney, by the way) but I have to admit that I know absolutely nothing about ghosts. I've written more than a few novels about them, but I don't *believe* in them. I believe that nothing happens after death but decay. Why, then, do I write about ghosts? Because I'm the first to admit I may be wrong about my disbeliefs and, secondly, if ghosts do exist they're probably very different from the way they're portrayed in literature and movies and on TV. We living human beings have a tendency to frame a mystery in familiar, comfortable terms, terms that have much to do with us and our expectations and predilections, much to do with how and why the mystery itself most appeals to us.

It's obvious that Greg Gifune has thought about the subject of ghosts quite a bit because the word portraits he paints of them in *A View from the Lake* make my imagination squirm. I'll let the author speak for himself:

And then through the darkness came the faces. The faces of children…or something like children, creations close but not quite exact, not quite perfect. They hovered around and above him, peering down at him with curiosity and a look of near delight.

Gifune chooses his words well, doesn't he? As I said earlier—he knows how to write. But are those actually ghosts he's writing about? Do ghosts inhabit *A View from the Lake* at all? Or is the author writing about something else, something nearly indefinable, something almost unknowable, something hellish that's nightmarishly not quite out of reach of us?

That's my little secret, because I've read the book. Twice. And as satisfying as it was the first time, it was even more satisfying the second time.

Perhaps I'll give it a third read. Correction, there's no "perhaps" about it; literature that absorbs us, that almost demands we read *every word*, is literature that, like great music, is always satisfying, always something to experience again and again.

Greg F. Gifune's *A View from the Lake* is that kind of literature.

Turn the page.

Start enjoying the great mysteries Greg Gifune has created.

T.M. Wright
March, 2010
Lindley, NY

"So she said nothing, but looked doggedly and sadly at the shore, wrapped in its mantle of peace; as if the people there had fallen asleep, she thought; were free to come and go like ghosts. They have no suffering there, she thought."
—Virginia Woolf
To the Lighthouse

CHAPTER ONE

She saw them only in dreams now. A young Japanese couple, the man tidy and stoic, the woman—his wife—petite and unassuming, a quiet sensuality concealed just below her studied exterior. Still as sculpture, the man would stand with his head bowed but eyes lifted, peering. James would emerge from surrounding shadows and crawl across the bare floor, nude and glistening with perspiration. The woman, inanimate as her husband, lay like a figurine with parted legs and sorrowful eyes, welcoming James with silence, thin lips moving soundlessly in prayer. James moved with an animal grace she did not remember him having in the real world, slithering over the woman, his pale buttocks gliding between the woman's legs as he tried to replace what had been taken, all that had been lost.

And the source of their loss, the little boy—such a beautiful child—his smile shy but genuine, young eyes full of wonder and awe, he was always there too. In short pants, matching jacket, neatly pressed oxford, flawless haircut and miniature dress shoes, he reminded her of a tiny businessman. But in her dreams he was detached, the same as her, forced to watch from a distance, already swallowed by darkness, already gone. Dead.

From a pair of glass sliders overlooking a large deck and enormous expanse of lake, Katherine sipped her coffee, hands clutching either side of the mug to absorb the warmth. She'd had the dream so many times that remembering it had little effect on her these days. Segments of it would cling to her like residue then dissipate over time as the day progressed, leaving her with only blurred and segmented visions.

A gentle but steady snow was falling, blowing about and blanketing Blissful Point in a sea of white. Frozen sheets of ice concealed the lake and hugged the weighted branches of trees along the portion of forest surrounding it. It had begun snowing the night before and had continued straight through to morning. The weather people on television had warned an enormous snowstorm was following behind this initial band of snow and that within the next twenty-four hours it would hit the area with a ferocity not seen in these parts since the infamous blizzard of 1978. A small Massachusetts town nestled amidst miles of woodland, in winter the population fell to less than five hundred residents. In summer it was an alternative to the more crowded Cape Cod vacation spots in the state, but the tourists who descended on the lake and filled the quaint little shops and cafés of the main street were little more than memories, as the locals dug in for what were always quiet and uneventful winter seasons. Most business properties sat boarded up and locked down, idle and silent, awaiting the return of summer. In winter, the village often looked as if it had been deserted, and on lonely days such as these, when snow and freezing temperatures kept even the year-round townies indoors, it might as well have been.

The woodstove in the corner of the small den crackled, filling the room with welcomed heat and the pleasant aroma of burning oak. The fire had gone out during the night, but now reborn, was quickly overtaking the chill Katherine had awakened to.

The main house where she lived was bookended by several small cottages all set back from the lakeshore and scattered amidst the sparse section of forest nearest the water. It had been twenty years since she and James had purchased the property and moved in, renting the cottages to tourists during the summer months and suffering the often-maddening solitude the remainder of the year offered.

And then, of course, there was the lake. Roosting there like some constant and dispassionate deity. Over the years she had grown to hate these cottages, this house, the grounds—with its picnic tables, rope-and-board swings, picturesque walking trails, bicycle paths carved into the forest landscape—and the lake.

Most of all she had grown to hate the lake.

When someone vanished without a trace, as James had done a little more than a year earlier, it didn't allow for the same levels of logic and closure certain death did.

Gone. That was the only tangible reality Katherine could be certain of. James was gone. To this day the authorities continued to consider him alive, as no body had been found and there was no evidence to suggest foul play or even suicide. But Katherine knew better. James was gone and he wasn't coming back. Ever.

James, you have to see a doctor, she had told him days before he vanished. *You have to get help, you have to stop this.*

With tears in his eyes, he had reached out and cupped the side of her face, gently stroking her cheek and smiling. *It's too late for that.*

And sadly, he'd been right.

Ironically, it was Katherine who wound up in therapy of sorts, seeking out Carlo Damone, an old college friend she'd stayed in touch with over the years. Carlo had originally set out to be a teacher, and although he'd graduated, he never got his teaching certification and instead went on to hold a string of menial jobs. In college he'd been the ultimate party guy—a hard-drinking and drug-taking madman, everyone's best friend and a social god—but when the party was over and real life came knocking, Carlo had never quite managed to adapt. In his twenties and thirties he'd bounced from one casual and unfulfilling relationship to the next, and though he'd moved briefly to Los Angeles he'd returned to Blissful Point within a year, broke and again seeking out a job to pay his rent. He was currently experiencing his longest stint in one job since they'd graduated college, and though it was only pumping gas at a local station downtown, this seemed to center him somewhat. Though a bit more stable, he often appeared as restless as ever, and still struggled with a drinking problem he'd had for the better part of two decades. But at least he now seemed resigned to staying put and getting himself together. Still, it was often difficult for Katherine to look long and hard at her old friend. Such promise and potential, and all of it reduced to a mere ember.

She remembered sitting in Carlo's latest digs—a tiny apartment above a small market in one of the less-appealing neighborhoods in town—and continuing to search for answers she suspected would forever linger just beyond her grasp. The state highway was so close the hum of traffic was often intrusive. "I'll never understand how you deal with the noise here."

"I like the noise, keeps my mind busy." He smiled playfully. "Hey, at least the rent's cheap. And I have an old friend that lives nearby."

"What's left of me anyway."

"Lot more left of you than there is of me," he said flatly.

"Is that supposed to make me feel better?"

This time Carlo's face showed no reaction, but his sad brown eyes gazed at her over half-glasses resting on the bridge of his nose. He'd been reading when she showed up and had apparently forgotten they were there. His vanity had never before allowed her to actually see him wearing them. "Real quiet out at the lake these days?"

"Yes, it is, but I won't be there much longer."

Carlo formed a chapel with his hands and let his chin rest at the summit where his fingers met. "I think it's definitely a good idea for you to try to start again somewhere else, but under the circumstances, Kate, are you sure that's the best way for you to deal with what's happened?"

"You're not honestly suggesting I stay there?"

"Not to the detriment of your health and wellbeing, no. I'm just saying running is never the answer."

Katherine could not be so sure.

"Believe me," he added, "I know, I've done it most of my life."

Memories of the authorities dragging the lake and how she'd stood in front of these same sliders watching the search and rescue recovery teams systematically hunt for James filtered through her mind. Miles of forest were scoured but no trace of him was found. The whisperings in town that he had gone mad gave birth to numerous theories regarding what may have happened to him, the most popular of which suggested he'd wandered off into the dense woods and up into the mountains where he became lost and eventually died. He was strange, people said, a poet and eccentric who kept to himself and rarely socialized with anyone other than his wife. But the people here had never really known her, much less James. There were also those who suspected her, the way spouses are always suspected first, but she dismissed those people and their rumors.

But for Carlo, and Marcy and Luke, a local couple Katherine and

James had been friendly with for several years, they had few friends or acquaintances they socialized with, and thus a very small circle of people who knew them in anything beyond the most facile sense. Marcy and Luke had divorced a few years earlier when Luke, an attorney, had taken up with his secretary and promptly moved out of town. Though their days of socializing as a couple were over, Marcy had remained friendly with Katherine and had been there for her during those horrible days after the disappearance. Only two years younger than Katherine, Marcy too now lived alone, as her only child Samantha, at twenty-one, had moved in with a boyfriend in Boston.

Marcy and Carlo had both been there for her as best they could, and she loved them for it. But in the end, Katherine still felt very much alone in her post-James existence. Alone in the darkness that had stolen him, in the darkness he had left behind.

Still, Katherine did her best to remember that they hadn't always been surrounded by such morbidity. In fact, the first few years they had taken up residence on the lake had been wonderful.

The madness had only begun once the lake had taken the child.

James had found the body in the early morning hours, floating facedown near the small pier from which he had fallen. Apparently the child had left the cabin his parents were renting and had wandered out to the lake in the middle of the night. Police speculated that in the dark he had fallen from the pier, struck his head and drowned in the shallow water just feet from shore.

James was never the same. Always a sensitive soul, the death of the young Japanese boy was something he was never able to recover from. And Katherine's visions of him kneeling in the sand, moaning through tears, the boy's tiny body clutched in his arms, lifelessly dangling there like some unattended puppet, had burned itself into her subconscious for eternity.

Months later, with fear and uncertainty, James would say, *I can't seem to focus. Do you understand? I can't focus. I—I can't stop it.*

It's not your fault, she had assured him repeatedly. *They were responsible for watching their own child. It was a tragedy, but you—we—did nothing wrong.*

James had smiled in a way she had never seen him smile before. Like he knew something she didn't. Many, many things.

For weeks before he disappeared he'd begun speaking to her in cryptic phrases and mutterings, as if convinced she knew what he was talking about.

Sweetie, she'd finally said, *you say things to me the way you'd say them if you were talking to yourself, as if I can understand without any explanation, as if I'm inside your head.*

You don't ever want to be there, James had said. *Not ever.*

And he was right.

Even a year and a half after his disappearance, most tourists didn't want to patronize a resort where first a child had drowned and then the proprietor had vanished without explanation a few months later. But for a few stragglers during the summer prior, the cottages had remained vacant and become rundown with neglect. What had once been a picturesque and charming little area was reduced to memories and fog.

"A large real estate developer made an offer on the property," she'd told Carlo on her last visit to see him. "Quite a substantial offer, actually."

He finally realized his reading glasses were still on and pulled them off. "Are you going to take it?" he asked, placing the glasses on a small table covered with assorted dog-eared paperbacks and notebooks.

"It's too much money to pass up." She assumed he would ask another question. When he didn't, she said, "Besides, there's nothing holding me there now, nothing to tie me to the lake. Sometimes I wonder if the whole thing wasn't cursed from the beginning."

Carlo said nothing, aware that she was referring to how she and her husband had managed to purchase such an expensive piece of real estate in the first place. Katherine's father had died when she was in high school, and though they were a working-class family, he had been heavily insured. Her mother had inherited nearly three hundred thousand dollars, and when a few years later she died from lung cancer, the remaining funds were left to Katherine, her only child. Most of it had gone toward the purchase of the lake.

"If it hadn't been for the deaths of my parents, we would've never been at the lake."

"But you did end up there," Carlo reminded her. "You can't second-guess things that have already happened."

"Aren't those the only things you *can* second-guess?" She tried to smile but it was hardly convincing. "I know it sounds melodramatic, but I even researched the history of the lake and woodlands. I don't know what I was hoping to find, a record of other horrible things happening here over the years maybe, who knows?"

"An actual curse, huh?" Carlo grinned playfully. "Any luck with that?"

"You're such a wiseass." She flashed a smirk of her own. "There was no record of anything ever happening at the lake. It was built back in the 1940s and there wasn't a single incident in all those years. Not a drowning or a death, which in itself almost seems suspect, but it's true. It's always been a quiet and fairly profitable little lakeside resort, all of it painfully uneventful. At least until that little boy drowned."

"You didn't really expect to find anything different, did you?"

"I guess not." She sighed absently. "I mean, no, of course not. At any rate, if all goes well I'll sign the papers next month and just sell it all off. I've finally begun to imagine life beyond that place for the first time in years. I retain residency through this winter but I'll have to be out by spring so workers can begin demolishing the cottages and clearing forest. Again, assuming the deal goes through. They plan to build a lakeside shopping center. Awful, I know, but I have to let these things, this place, go."

The sun was setting, darkening Carlo's apartment. A shadow crept across the room like the thief it was. "It's understandable that you'd be a little freaked out with their plans. The lake's been your home for a long time."

"But I can't concern myself with that now. I'll be gone, and I won't be going back."

She hadn't yet decided exactly where she'd go, but despite Carlo's concerns, she felt the only hope for a normal life again depended on her ability to start over elsewhere. At the end of the day, proverbial and otherwise, the only thing she knew for sure was that this would be her last season there.

"One more winter," she said softly, "one more winter on the lake."

CHAPTER TWO

Katherine stepped closer to the sliders, sipped more coffee and continued to watch the snowfall. She remembered that last time she'd visited Carlo's apartment, and how it was always so cramped in there, as if the walls were just waiting to snap shut on her like some giant mousetrap. It had begun to rain as they discussed the theories behind the madness James had experienced. Katherine sat in her usual chair, watching the blurred windowpanes rather than her friend's noncommittal expression. The rhythm of the rain along the roof relaxed her, reminded her of times she would awaken on rainy mornings next to James and how the rain always made her feel safe and protected. "I've forgotten what it feels like," she said softly. "Feeling safe."

"You mean you feel unsafe?"

"There are days I do."

"Well, we all—"

"This is different."

"Why are you feeling unsafe then?"

"The madness."

"Madness in general or James's madness?"

Her eyes found him. "I'm beginning to think they're the same."

"How so?"

"Sometimes I think the madness he experienced has become mine too." She forced a smile and nonchalantly crossed her legs. "It sounds silly, I know, but—"

"Not really." Carlo let the silence linger awhile. "Actually, it's not that unusual for two people who have a strong connection—love, for example—to experience a shared psychosis. There have been specific case studies with married couples, for instance, examples where one began to suffer acute mental illness, and over time, as the partner attempted to care for the one afflicted, he or she too began to suffer from identical or curiously similar symptoms, the same illness, as it were."

This time when Katherine smiled it was not forced. "Contagious insanity?"

"That's an interesting way to phrase it," Carlo said, "but in a sense, yeah. Sometimes when the love or emotional connection between two people is so intense, their emotions can reach beyond traditional forms of understanding and empathy and into a realm where what is real and what is only in the mind, so to speak, become one in the same or so similar it's difficult to find a discernable difference. To the subject, that is."

"So if two people can transfer madness from one to the other—"

"Well, that's not what I said, I—"

"But if one were to become insane and the other loved that person so deeply that they could literally share their insanity—assume it, in a sense—how much further would you have to go to take that concept to its logical conclusion?"

Carlo seemed wholly amused. "And what would that be?"

"Wouldn't it also make sense to at least consider that the illness might be something more than a condition? Wouldn't it redefine insanity—or at least that particular, specific form of it—change it from some disease lurking in the depths of a tortured mind into something more tangible? Wouldn't it—*couldn't* it—make it real, literal, rather than conceptual?"

Carlo gave a subtle nod. "I assume you mean to the person experiencing it?"

She had not meant that at all but rather than correct him she continued with her train of thought. "And if that were true, then what would become of it once the source, the conduit through which the madness was originally born, ceased to exist? Where would the madness go? Would it lie dormant, waiting for the opportune time to show itself? Would it manifest itself at all? And if it did, how—and when?"

Katherine left her chair. There was something freeing about movement, about space. It felt good to be standing by the two tall windows on the far wall, watching the rain through aged sheer curtains. Carlo hadn't said a word since she'd stood up, but she could feel him watching, studying her.

"You haven't answered," she finally said.

"About where madness goes once its host is gone?" He smiled. "Well, I'm not a psychiatrist, Katherine. I'm not even a psychologist. Christ, I pump gas for a living."

"And what a waste that is," she said sadly.

"True, but it is honest work, and since we're talking about you, let's stick to that. So, as a gas-pumping professional, this is only layman conjecture, of course, but a belief in the premise that—"

"You don't believe the illness James experienced might somehow now be attempting to become *my* experience?"

"I think you might want to consider that you're assigning emotion and human traits to something void of either."

"But that in itself is an assumption, Carlo."

"But a fairly safe one, don't you think?" His eyebrows arched up the way they often did when he was attempting to be ironic. "Look, it might be better to assign those emotions to yourself, as something shared between you and James. Guilt, for example, you mentioned James had this tremendous guilt over the drowning death of the boy."

From the second-floor apartment Katherine could see the street below, a ragged public basketball court to the north, and in the distance beyond, the state highway. She focused on the car headlights, blurred by the rain, and wondered about the people behind each wheel, who they were, where they were going, and why. So many lives being waged in haphazard unison, connected yet solitary. "He did feel a lot of guilt," she answered.

"And you?"

"No." She looked over her shoulder at him, sitting in his rummage-sale recliner. Though not unattractive, poor Carlo seemed perpetually self-conscious—uncomfortable in his own skin—in a subtle but unmistakable manner. She adored her old friend, and it had been so long since she'd had the chance to immerse herself in a genuine, intelligent and provocative conversation, but sometimes Carlo came across so lonely and isolated she often felt guilty discussing her problems while seldom inquiring about his own. "The boy wandered off from the cabin in the middle of the night, we had no control over that. I felt badly that he died, of course, but I didn't feel guilty. My heart broke for the parents. They were vacationing in the United States for the first time and spoke very limited English. Before it all happened they were very polite, formal, and the little boy was so innocent and beautiful, always smiling." She turned back to the window, back to the rain and the cars and the faceless phantoms imprisoned within them. "The parents were devastated, but they maintained this sense of etiquette and restraint that was amazing to me. In some ways it angered me because I got the impression the man in particular was behaving as if their child had shamed them somehow—by drowning, for God's sake. It was a cultural thing, I suppose, something I couldn't understand but... their child was dead, I had no right to judge them or interpret their grief. All they wanted to do was take their little boy and go home, and who could blame them?"

"It's so hideous when a child dies the mind just shuts down at the thought of it."

The sound of Carlo's voice again distracted her from the rain. "James was never the same after that little boy drowned." She reached out, touched the cool window glass and watched the rain on the other side glide between her fingers. "He spent even more time alone, like he was purposely segregating himself from the world. He wrote in his journal constantly, but he stopped reading his work to me, his poems. He became protective of his journal and paranoid of my reading it. I had to continually tell him I had no interest in reading it unless he wanted me to."

"Did James believe you?"

"I don't know. I don't think so."

"Did you ever read the journal?"

"No, it disappeared with him."

"You were saying James was never the same after the boy drowned."

"He became distant, cold, more so than he'd been prior."

Carlo sighed softly. "I don't exactly think it's a stretch to suggest that there was always a bit of coldness to James."

"Not a coldness, really, but a—a bit of a wall, I suppose. You knew him, Carlo, I—"

"I don't think I *knew* him, particularly."

"We were all friends, I'm just saying—"

"You and I are friends, Katherine. James and I were, at best, acquaintances."

"But you knew him, that's what I'm getting at. As warm and wonderful as James could sometimes be, there were other times when he was remote and somewhat cold."

"That's true of everyone to a degree, but maybe a bit more so when it came to James."

Katherine nodded.

"What about you? Do you believe *you* knew James very well?"

The question should have offended her, but it didn't. "We were married for years, so of course I'd like to think so. But from the time we met we were a bit of an odd couple. Then again, it was right after college and that's an awkward transitional time for nearly everyone. We just seemed to click. Maybe it was because we were both English majors."

"I didn't major in English, and you and I got along great."

"You got along great with everyone," she said, smiling as she remembered the college version of Carlo, the slightly thinner version, with more hair—a lot more hair—long and wild like a rock star, the dangle earring and the then bright smile, a roguish smile that made you feel like he was tap-dancing on the edge but that everything would be all right as long as you stuck with him. "You were always the life of the party."

"But you and I were close, that's what I meant. And still are, despite our differences."

"It's not the same though."

"Yeah, I—you're right." Carlo nodded clumsily and looked away.

"And besides," she said, "you first met him right around that same time and thought he was a strange choice. I could tell."

"Well, I never—"

"It's all right. Like you, I was still considering teaching in those days and James was focused on being a poet and author, so we had different plans at that point, but he was always eccentric."

"All artists are. Shit, nothing wrong with that, I'm an accomplished eccentric myself."

"So it wasn't his eccentricity then?"

Carlo shook his head in the negative.

"What then?"

He hesitated a moment, thinking his answer through. "In my

eyes, I guess nobody was ever quite good enough for you."

She smiled even though her back was to him. "You're the sweetest person I know."

"Now *that's* depressing."

Katherine removed her hand from the window and studied the lines crisscrossing her palm. They reminded her of barbed wire.

Stay away from the windows, James had told her days before his disappearance. *They can see you.*

Who, James? There's no one there, sweetheart, no one watching.

He's crawling around. That's what they do, but they can still see us from there.

What are you talking about? From where?

His lips had trembled into a grimace as he pointed through the window to the lake. *There.*

She pushed the memories of him away, swept them into darkness. "I knew James from a very particular and personal perspective," Katherine told him. "But sometimes it was as if his life began when he met me, as if his past, his life before me, before us, was something totally separate, an entirely different life."

"Maybe it was," Carlo said. "How much do you really know about his past?"

"James rarely spoke about his life before us. I know the basics. He was originally from the western part of the state. He was put up for adoption by his birth mother, who he never knew, and was raised in a series of foster homes. One couple in particular, the Covingtons, raised him from the time he was nine until he turned eighteen. He referred to them as his 'parents' but they weren't close at all. They didn't even attend our wedding."

"I was going to say I didn't remember them being there."

"James didn't really want them there and I doubt they wanted to attend anyway, so I never interfered. His childhood was a touchy subject for him, he could be sensitive about it, and who could blame him?"

"Did you ever meet these people?"

"Only once, and it was very briefly a few weeks before we were married. He rarely saw them or even spoke with them on the telephone. They just weren't a part of his life after he turned eighteen and moved out, and in the end, I got the impression that was just fine with both sides. The one time I met them was the only time I ever spoke to either of them, and that was twenty years ago."

"Sounds like an awkward situation."

"It was." Katherine nodded. "They were really odd together, this mismatched older couple and their foster son. There was a distance between them, a kind of formality that was a bit unnerving. It was clear they weren't that comfortable around each other."

"It's sad," Carlo said. "I mean, that was the only family the guy had."

"Yes, until he met me." Katherine remained quiet awhile. "They were from a small rural town in the western part of the state, simple people who struck me as really uncomfortable out of their element, which constituted nearly everywhere other than their own hometown. His foster father, Darren was his name, was this tall, razor-thin guy with really pointed features. Like a bird, you know what I mean? He worked as a mechanic if I remember correctly. He was one of those quiet and reserved types, but almost to the point of being comatose. His foster mother Josephine was a housewife, but I remember she worked part-time as a teacher's aide or something along those lines, something with kids. She seemed very aloof to me, but also seemed to carry around a lot of resentment too. When I met her I couldn't be sure if that was directed toward James, me, or the world in general. Later James assured me it was the latter. She just seemed like one of those people that life and time leaves bitter and angry, you know?"

"I'm vaguely familiar with the concept."

"So am I…now."

"You only met and spoke to them that one time then? You didn't contact them after James disappeared?"

"No, as I say, I haven't seen them in twenty years and they hadn't been a part of James's life in all that time so it seemed unlikely they'd know anything about his disappearance. And it seemed even more unlikely to me that James might contact them. But even if I'd wanted to I wasn't sure how to locate them. I know Darren died a few years ago, I remember James got a call from Josephine one day while I was out. He was surprised to have heard from her, actually. He said something about Josephine planning to move to some small town in Rhode Island—apparently that's where she'd grown up—but I don't know what town it was. The thought of trying to find her to see if she'd heard from him or knew anything else did actually cross my mind but only briefly, because as I mentioned, I thought the odds were very low that she'd know anything, and I wasn't even sure where to find her or if she was even still alive herself. She was an older woman when I met her two decades ago, for God's sake."

"Do you know if the police contacted them after the disappearance?"

"Not to my knowledge, but I can't say for sure. I tend to doubt it."

Carlo let their lingering thoughts die down a bit before speaking again. "I certainly didn't know James well, but he usually seemed to be a really sweet guy."

"He could be."

"But he also was a hard person to get close to. As you say, he had walls."

"Thicker than most, you're right." She sighed long and hard. "Carlo, I knew James as well as anyone did or ever had, but there was this point with him I was never able to penetrate either. No one could. That's true of everyone to some extent, though. No one ever knows anyone else completely, utterly. None of us are ever totally revealed."

"That's because nobody's ever completely what they seem to be," Carlo said. "We all keep secrets."

Katherine turned back to him and gave a slow nod. "And we all tell lies."

"Even you?"

"Even me."

"Even James?"

"*Especially* James."

CHAPTER THREE

Katherine watched the snow gradually blanket the cabins, the flakes radiant in the morning light, graceful as falling ash. It reminded her of a poem James had written long ago, one of her favorites about snow being like intricate splinters of glass, pieces from a delicate crystal globe mishandled by the gods and dropped, shattered in the heavens, the remnants of which silently fell to Earth.

There had once been a genuine purity to James, a sense of wonder many artists possess, but that was so very long ago she often had trouble remembering that version of her husband. Those broken pieces of curiously beautiful glass he had once written about with innocent, childlike awe had turned to raindrops of fire, a cancerous plague he could not outrun.

Her memories returned to Carlo. He'd sat up the moment she mentioned James's harbored secrets, her comment stirring in him a level of curiosity he had not shown previously. *"Especially* James?" he asked, repeating it back to her. "Why do you say that?"

"Because what we're really talking about is the true nature of people, isn't it?" He answered her with another quizzical look, so she said, "And since his disappearance I've come to the conclusion that the true nature of James was hidden more deeply than most." Her eyes bounced about the apartment, hoping for something to catch and hold her attention. Something was attempting to distract her now, an unseen something she could not explain but could feel to the depths of her being.

He's here, James had told her again and again, jotting endless notes and entries in his journal, pressing it against his chest whenever she was close enough to read it over his shoulder. *Even when I can't see or feel him, he's here. He's here and…I don't think he's alone.*

The boy, James? The little boy? He's dead.

I know.

"I think he was seeing the boy again."

"The little Japanese boy?"

"Yes."

Carlo cleared his throat. "All right."

"He never actually said it but he kept referring to seeing someone, someone who was watching him. I took it to be the boy. Like he was having hallucinations or psychotic memories or God knows what."

Carlo crossed his legs, let his chin rest in the palm of one hand and said, "You said James was pretty badly traumatized at finding the boy's dead body, and that he started having these problems not long afterward. You said he was racked with guilt, which seems like an odd emotion to experience under the circumstances."

"But that was the way James saw things. He was a control freak, and in his mind he felt he had somehow failed to provide a safe environment for this child."

"But you did provide a safe environment. The boy's death had nothing to do with the lake or the cabins being unsafe or—"

"Of course not, but this is how James felt. He felt he should've been able to do something to prevent it. It's just the way he was."

"But you're telling me you think that in some emotionally, mentally damaged fog he started actually *seeing* this kid again?"

Katherine nodded slowly.

"And we're not talking about dreams or nightmares, right? You're talking waking, lucid moments here, yes?"

"Yes."

"Okay look, there's no graceful way to ask this so I'm just going to throw it out there. You don't think James had something to do with the boy's death, do you?"

"No," she said quickly. "He was with me in bed that night. I was awake before James was the morning he found the body. We'd been in bed for a while, awake but quiet."

"But it's possible he could've been up before that then gone back to bed before—"

"I don't believe James was even remotely capable of that level of violence."

"Okay." Carlo seemed to relax a bit. "Good. I didn't think so but I had to ask."

"James wouldn't hurt a fly. This was a man that carried bugs outside rather than step on them. He was the gentlest person I've ever known."

"Yeah, I know. I'm sorry for even—"

"It's all right," she said evenly. "It's not as if the thought never crossed my mind."

It all seemed so staged here, in Carlo's little apartment, so studied, interchangeable, empty and lifeless. No particular point or meaning, just a messy shamble of existence, disorganized and nearly hopeless, like so much of life these days, like so much she and everyone else had trained themselves to simply ignore, to blank out rather than confront. With selective vision and a filtered consciousness, the world, it seemed, had drifted off to sleep. It was as if she were the only one still awake in a universe of dreams. As quirky and distinctive as Carlo was, even he had seemed to melt into the landscape, here in his cluttered and thoroughly impassive apartment.

He'd been a dreamer once. Now, like this place, he was broken and tired and worn.

"At first I wondered if it was that goddamn lake," she said, "if it were to blame, if it somehow was a malevolent force we couldn't or didn't want to understand. I know that sounds absurd but James used to sit and stare at it for hours, especially toward the end. But then I remembered he once told me he believed we were all sleepwalking, and that people were haunted, not places or things because places and things had become far too uninteresting, and all that remained was what we *didn't* want to see, what we *didn't* want to know about ourselves."

"What do you think he meant by that?"

"In one of his poems, one of the last ones he wrote and let me read, I remember a line that read: 'Confronting our own black places are all that remains in an otherwise soulless world.'" Katherine laughed bitterly. "In his own way—however pretentious—I realize now that he was making a confession."

Carlo nibbled his thumbnail—an unattractive nervous habit he'd had since she'd known him—and leaned forward in his chair, as if afraid he might otherwise miss something. "And what was he confessing to?"

"His true nature maybe?"

"Which is?"

"Was."

"But you don't know for sure if James is dead."

"He's gone. I can feel it."

"You sense he's dead?"

She glanced at him without ever making direct eye contact. "I said gone, not dead."

"Then you think he's still alive?"

"Not necessarily."

This time Carlo's face betrayed him, and a baffled expression appeared before he could stifle it. "You lost me, babe, I don't understand."

A faint smile tickled her upper lip. "I know you don't."

"All right, I'll do my best to keep up," he said, returning her insincere smile with one of his own. "Go on."

"Near the end he was terrified, but not of death. At least not death like we know it, or think we know it. It was like he knew he was going to leave, to disappear, it was a decision he'd made. But it was as if he wasn't totally in control of it. Whatever it was…or is." Katherine clasped her hands together to prevent the trembling her memories of him always caused. "It was as if he knew he had to go but wasn't quite sure where, or how exactly he might do it. I don't know, it—it's just a theory."

"Tell me more about that," Carlo said. "This theory, I mean."

"The darkness," she said, turning away, "the madness—whatever we'd like to call it, once confronted, became something more than mere mental illness for him. He started reading all these books on the nature of reality and existence. He'd spend hours studying books on parapsychology, religion and psychic phenomenon. He was consumed, like he was looking for an answer to what was happening to him, but was running out of time."

Carlo refrained from comment for a moment then said, "Do you think James found in these things any of the answers he was looking for?"

"No."

"Some solace maybe?"

"No."

"It was just a dead end then?"

"Life itself had become a dead end for James."

"Happens to the best of us."

She let his comment pass. "It was like he'd backed into a corner and the way into that corner had been sealed off behind him. He was trapped."

Sometimes I wonder if he realizes I know he's there, James had said in the final days of his existence, when for him sanity had become tattered and useless. *He's quiet, very, very quiet,* he'd said with a smile somewhere between frenzied and triumphant, *but I know when he's there. I feel him.*

"What was broken—damaged—in his mind," she explained, "became real to him. His work was always somewhat dark and sinister, his poems always morbid, and at some point they began to consume him. They became his reality."

"*His* reality, I see." Carlo did his best to appear solicitous. "And you?"

"What about me?"

"Are these things that consumed him becoming your reality too?"

Katherine took a final look at Carlo's apartment, the window, and hoped this was the last time she'd ever have to come here. Though she loved her old friend dearly, there was no point returning to this musty old place ever again. She could see him elsewhere. "I was hoping you could tell me."

CHAPTER FOUR

Katherine shook a cigarette free from her pack, rolled it into the corner of her mouth and left it dangling while she searched her robe pocket for a lighter. The snow continued to fall, the world beyond the sliders a growing blur of white.

Once found, she ignited the lighter, lit her cigarette then snapped it shut. She took a deep drag, exhaled with a sigh and through the slow spiral of smoke, watched the dark cabins and the stretch of land beside them. Just beyond, the lake lay frozen and barely visible through a snowflake ballet.

With cigarette in one hand and a gradually cooling mug of coffee in the other, she stared through the snow to the past; saw James long before the madness. They had been together for two years and had only recently purchased the lake property. *Twenty-five. My God,* she thought, *we were only twenty-five.*

The snow melted away, replaced by green grass and a warm breeze rolling in off the lake. The sun was still setting, a radiant ember on the horizon just above the distant trees. James sat naked on the bank of the lake, taking in the world around him as he often did, his body wet and dripping from a recent swim. But for occasionally shooing away a mosquito, his body remained extraordinarily still. Never one to kill even a bug, he would remove them from his body with a gentle flick of his finger then watch them fly off the way a child or an unusually perceptive adult watches something similar, like the flight of a butterfly. Boundless wonder and awe, such a beautiful thing in a grown man, Katherine thought, and so rare, so very rare.

She watched him age, there on the sandy edges of the lake.

Ten years later. Ten years ago. Thirty-five now. Still so young, the both of them, and James, still christening the lake at the start of each season with a skinny dip a week or so before the tourists arrived.

A ritual he had established in their first year there, always a creature of habit, he refused to let it go. He would stroll about naked the way a toddler might, unaware and in possession of innocence she could only envy. Katherine, always more reserved, would sit and watch her husband, content to eventually join him for a swim in her bathing suit or a pair of cut-offs and a T-shirt. Now and then she'd swim topless with him, but she'd never felt wholly comfortable being bottomless as well, always afraid someone might appear unannounced, intrude on their privacy and embarrass her.

Barney, just a kitten then, hopped along the grass, chased first his tail in a furious frenzy of spinning maneuvers then zeroed in on James and began stalking him with delusions of grandeur, slinking about like a lion hunting on the Serengeti. James pretended not to see, and when the tiny puff eventually pounced, he laughed and scooped the kitten up in his hands, kissing his nose as they rolled about in the grass.

Katherine looked to the garden. She had still tended one in those days. Things were still growing then, *they* were still growing then, ten years married and as much in love as ever, with their small lake resort and their kitten and moments like these. Beautiful things still bloomed. The world had not yet turned dark. James had not yet gone hopelessly insane.

But even then, on that wonderful quiet afternoon, she knew they would probably never again be so happy. Life was not that generous. There was always a price to pay, even for temporary moments of bliss.

Prices paid reminded her of Carlo, and that final time she'd met with him at his apartment. He'd risen from his chair, slipped into the kitchen then returned with a bottle of whiskey and two glasses. "Have you talked with Marcy about all this?" Carlo asked.

"Not to the same depths we have, no. I mean, Marcy wants me to go see a *psychic*, for God's sake."

"She can't be serious."

"She swears by this guy, says he's told her all sorts of things."

"Oh come on, Katherine, don't tell me you're buying into that nonsense these days."

"No, not really, but I guess I try to keep an open mind."

"The key is for your mind to be open but still functioning logically."

"It's not like I have anything to lose."

"You're actually going to let her drag you to a psychic then?"

"Probably," she said with a chuckle. "She's just trying to help, Carlo."

"I know she is—hell, I like Marcy too but—"

"That's not what you said when you dated her," Katherine reminded him.

The statement stopped Carlo cold for a moment. "You're the one that insisted I go out with her."

"You were both single, alone and unattached. I thought—"

"It's not that I didn't like her, Katherine. I did, and still do. But we made better friends than anything else, and after two dates that was clear to both of us." Carlo drew a deep breath, let it out slowly. "Look, Marcy's a hot shit and a good person, and she's been a loyal friend to you, but I think if you want answers about James there are better ways to—"

"I know, I know. I just figure if I go and get it over with she'll stop bugging me about it. Marcy's a little ditsy but—"

"Marcy's a lot ditsy," he said with a grin.

"But she means well."

"Don't we all?" He set the glasses on the coffee table and spun the cap off the bottle.

"I think what we need is a drink."

Katherine nodded without looking at him. In college she'd been more of a drinker, though unlike Carlo, she'd cut back significantly upon joining the real world. He'd kept right on, adding alcoholism to his already growing list of problems. But then she enjoyed the luxury of restraint. He did not. James, on the other hand, had never been much of drinker. He rarely drank and had never done drugs, even in college when she and Carlo and virtually everyone else had smoked pot and dabbled with an array of other substances from time to time.

"Here, it'll make you feel better," Carlo said, thrusting a glass at her.

"Is that what it does for you, Carlo?"

"Just take the fucking drink, Katherine."

She offered a mock salute before accepting the glass.

Carlo bowed his head like a sorrowful child. "I'm sorry, I didn't mean to…"

"It's okay." She gave his shoulder a gentle squeeze. "I'm sorry too. Here you are listening to my problems and I start preaching to you. I just…you know I worry."

"And I appreciate it, but don't sweat it." He raised his glass. "You know me, baby, I'm indestructible."

Katherine clicked her glass against his. "To better days."

"Just so long as they don't get any worse," he said with a wink. They each took a sip of whiskey.

"It's a bit harsh," she said, her throat constricting.

"Sorry, can't swing the good stuff these days."

After a beat she said, "Have you given any thought to your own plans for the future?"

He smiled, but it was distinctly sorrowful. "You mean in terms of getting some direction or point to this miserable existence I try to pass off as a life?"

"That's not what I meant and you know it."

"I'll get it together," he said softly. "I will, I—I promise I will."

She watched him a moment, reminded of how when she was just a teenager herself she'd come across a lost little boy in a department store. The child had somehow become separated from his parents and was terrified. Standing alone in an aisle, he'd not quite been crying but had a look of such horror and barely controlled emotion he seemed dangerously close to a complete breakdown at any second. While all had turned out well—Katherine had comforted the child and taken him to a customer service desk where his parents were frantically in the process of reporting him missing—the look in that little boy's eyes was something she had never forgotten. Such a hopeless look of being lost, alone and afraid, the same look she'd found in Carlo's eyes ever since their college days, which now encompassed the vast majority of his adult life.

"You're my oldest and dearest friend," she told him. "I don't want to lose you too."

"You won't." Carlo finished his drink in a quick gulp, returned to the coffee table and grabbed the bottle. "Look, instead of wasting your time worrying about me and going to psychics with Marcy, why don't you let me help you?"

"You are helping," she said through a thin smile.

"No, I mean really help." He poured himself another drink. "I've got a lot of free time these days."

Katherine turned back to the window, the rain. "What did you have in mind?"

"Maybe I could look into James for you, his background and whatnot. I know a lot of his past is kind of murky, but maybe there's something there that might—"

"I don't think there was anything terribly interesting about his past, Carlo. I think he just chose not to talk about it a lot because it was difficult for him."

"I'm just saying, maybe I can come up with some useful information."

"I don't know that there's anything *to* find."

"Right, you don't know. That's the point."

"Somehow, I don't think the whole detective thing quite works for you." She sipped her drink. "But thanks."

"If you change your mind, I'm willing to look into it for you."

Quiet fell over the small apartment. Only the rain sounds continued.

"I could call Reggie Byers," Carlo added.

"Reggie?" she asked, memories of their old college friend flashing in her tired mind.

"Haven't spoken to him in years, but if he's still with the state police he can help."

"God, I haven't seen Reggie since school. I wonder how he's doing."

"Last I heard he was living in Boston, still married to Debbie and had a couple kids."

Katherine shrugged. "I'm not sure I want to involve him in all this."

"Why don't you just let me see what I can come up with? I—hell, if nothing else, it'll give me something to do besides sit around and drink."

"I'll think about it, okay?"

"Let me be useful for a while," Carlo said. "Please, let me do this."

Only silence answered for what seemed a very long time.

"We'll see," Katherine finally said. "We'll see."

Something soft brushed her leg, bringing her back to the here and now, to the snow.

Katherine glanced down to see Barney slinking between her ankles, rubbing his hindquarters along her calves and purring with delight. He'd only recently again begun to do such things. After James vanished he had sat near the sliders or in the windows for hours on end, watching the grounds, waiting for his return. Always a happy cat, Barney had become more withdrawn and sullen since the loss of James, mourning him the same as Katherine had.

She smiled, crouched down and ran a hand across his back. It was good to see him happy again, like a kitten.

Barney enjoyed her touch, craning his neck so his head could meet her fingers, his purr increasing in volume as he moved gracefully back and forth between her feet.

Without warning he recoiled, snapped his head toward the slider and sat at attention. His green eyes narrowed, watching and waiting as a low, barely audible growl emanated from deep in his throat.

Fighting off a sudden chill, Katherine turned back to the sliders.

Through the swirling flakes of snow, a figure emerged. Walking slowly down the path between the lake and the grounds was a lone man dressed in a long dark overcoat and a black knit hat. Katherine put her coffee down, quickly butted her cigarette in an ashtray and moved toward one end of the sliders. She cocked her head in an attempt to see the modest parking area between her house and the next cottage, but it revealed only her old Ford Bronco.

It was virtually unheard of to see a stranger this time of year, particularly on foot.

The man was at the base of the steps now. He glanced in both directions then lifted a pair of black eyes to the sliders, his lips pursed, trails of mist tumbling from his nostrils as his breath hit the frigid air.

As she held his dead stare, Katherine felt another chill trickle across her spine. She did her best to appear unaffected. "Can I help you?" she asked, raising her voice so it could be heard through the glass. The man stared at her but offered no response. "This is private property, can I help you?" Katherine closed her robe at the neck with one hand and cinched the belt tightly around her waist with the other. Her unexpected visitor stood mere feet from her, separated only by a few steps and the large pane of glass. His rugged and heavily lined face made it difficult for her to gauge his age.

"Nothing's moving in the snow," the man said, his voice gravelly and tight, as if he rarely used it. "The roads are getting worse."

It was certainly an odd way to begin a conversation, but she assumed he had seen the old sign advertising cottages for rent. Still, what was this man doing in a tourist town not only in the middle of winter but also with one of the worst snowstorms the area had seen in years on its way and already beginning to bear down? She leaned a bit closer to the slider. "I'm sorry, but we're no longer in business."

"It's very cold."

"You don't understand. I can't rent anymore, we're closed."

"It's very cold," the man said again.

Katherine glanced at the slider to make certain it was locked. "If you get back on the main road and—"

The man shook his head and motioned in the direction from which he'd come. A little girl stood huddled in a winter coat, the hood pulled up over her head so that her face was hidden. From her physical stature she appeared to be no more than six or seven years old. "She's only a child," he said in monotone.

Katherine sidestepped a wave of guilt. "Where's your car?"

The man said nothing, only stared at her as if he hadn't understood the question.

His behavior seemed odd at best, wildly suspicious at worst. But then, what if he was simply disoriented? They had to have a car in such a desolate location. Maybe they'd had an accident. Or maybe he was some deranged lunatic.

Or just maybe, she thought, *I'm being paranoid.*

Hadn't she once accused James of the same indiscretion when he'd first begun to question everything he saw and heard? Every excuse in the world, every rationalization was attempted, but once acknowledged nothing could stop it, nothing could make those things that haunted him go away.

Now it was a daily struggle to make certain they did not haunt her as well.

The lake had done this to her—to them both—it had all started with the lake, always the goddamn lake. It had caused her to never be quite sure which emotions were real and which were imagined. It had taken so much from her and left her with so little, most days it was impossible to distinguish genuine feelings of fear, loss and confusion with the incoherent ramblings that often coursed through her mind.

Although she felt horrible turning them away, she was a woman in the middle of nowhere and had little choice. If the man was not prepared to better explain his circumstances, then she was in no position to trust him.

"I'm sorry," she said.

The man watched her silently, the falling snowflakes rapidly accumulating across his inert form. Not wanting him to realize she was alone, she glanced over her shoulder and pretended to call someone. "Honey, can you come out here a minute? Someone's here."

Katherine turned back to the deck, prepared to carry the bluff further, but the man and the little girl were gone.

CHAPTER FIVE

It wasn't possible. How could the man and the little girl have simply vanished into thin air? Katherine stepped closer to the sliders in an attempt to see as much of the property as possible, but they were nowhere in sight.

Voices whispered to her, sweeping through her mind like a breeze, indecipherable and ephemeral, gone before any sense could be made of them. She slowly backed away from the sliders, still holding her robe closed as if this might somehow protect her, and listened to the sound of her heart crashing against the walls of her chest. Had the man and little girl simply walked away, they would not have had time to get beyond her range of vision so quickly. Could the falling snow have masked their retreat? Katherine wondered. She looked deeper into the slowly mounting storm, watched the flakes swirl about. But there was nothing, no one there.

A chill crept along her spine and fanned out along the base of her neck and shoulders. Her fingers and toes tingled, and she moved her arms out from her body in a slow flapping motion to shake the pins and needles free.

You can't save yourself, Katherine. How could you have saved me?

"My God, James," she said gently, "is this how it was for you?"

It's all right, he'd told her, standing near these same sliders before he'd vanished, tears trickling along his face as he stared out into the night, seeing things no one else could. *It's me. I'm the one who has to go, don't you see? It's me, Kate. I'm the one.*

And now perhaps those same shadows wanted her as well.

No, she told herself. Goddamn it, no. James was insane. James was mentally ill and she was not. She assured herself again, eyes still searching for the trespassers, that she was perfectly rational. There had to be an explanation, a reasonable explanation. There had to be.

Can you hear it? James had asked once, more statement than question, his head cocked as he listened to the silence.

Hear what, James? Katherine had asked, desperate to hold back tears, to somehow reach him and pull him back from the precipice his madness had lured him to.

The footsteps, can you hear them?

She hadn't heard them, but now wondered if that too might soon change.

The only sounds that beckoned to her just then were memories of the night before, when she had finally given in and gone with Marcy to see Jacques, her psychic advisor. Marcy had shown up at Katherine's in her new SUV, a hulking vehicle that brought new meaning to the term ostentatious. Though she adored Marcy, Katherine often found her flamboyant nature and flashy exterior a bit embarrassing, as she was nothing like that herself, preferring to remain understated whenever possible. And yet, some small part of Katherine envied her friend's confidence and ability to draw attention so shamelessly.

"Hey!" Marcy screamed over the blaring stereo. "Can you believe this thing? I got the biggest, most expensive one they had on the lot!"

"My God, Marcy," Katherine said, struggling to climb into the monstrosity, "are you sure it's big enough?" Since she'd never been to see a psychic before, Katherine hadn't been sure what to wear, and as she fought her way into the SUV she was pleased she'd opted for jeans and a sweater.

"I went all out and got the eight-speaker CD system too!" To further emphasis this she cranked the volume to a point where the entire vehicle was vibrating to the strains of techno dance music. "It's like driving a tour bus," she yelled. "Isn't it scandalous?"

"I thought you were going to get something practical!" Katherine screamed back.

"I was but it'll piss Luke off knowing I bought something so over the top and unnecessary! I plan to keep right on spending the bastard's alimony as fast as he sends it to me. I was going for something really offensive and grotesque!"

Katherine reached over and turned the stereo down. "Mission accomplished."

"I've lived in places that weren't as nice as this." She grinned.

"At least it'll be good in the snow."

"It's truly awful," Katherine said, stifling a laugh. Though she was one of the sweetest people Katherine had ever known, Marcy possessed the kind of effervescence and frenetic energy generally reserved for speed freaks, and was someone for whom subtlety existed only as a vague concept. As if determined to prove this point, Marcy had dressed in a skin-tight leopard print top, an equally snug black skirt, black hose, trendy boots and a leather jacket—completely inappropriate considering the temperature and weather, but utterly Marcy. Her makeup was heavy, her hair styled and teased high like a rock groupie from the 1980s, and her fingernails were painted neon pink. Dangle diamond earrings, brilliant even in limited light, hung from each ear, and an array of gold necklaces and rings adorned her neck and fingers. Though forty-three, she still presented herself like a twenty-something party girl, and often got away with it, albeit at a distance.

"Now, I know you're nervous or whatever, but don't worry about tonight," she told Katherine. "Jacques is way cool and not spooky or creepy or anything. I met him at a psychic fair at the mall a few years ago and I've been going to him every few months ever since. Lots of people in town do, actually, but he has clients that come from all over New England to see him. He's really good if he gets the right energy from you, so just go with it and keep an open mind, okay?"

Katherine nodded helplessly.

"He's been doing this ever since he was in high school when he was visited by his spirit guides. They told him about this gift he had and that he should use it to help others, so that's what he's done ever since."

"Um, okay."

"I know, trippy, huh?" Marcy winked and smiled knowingly. "Just wait, you'll see."

Jacques—no last name, just *Jacques*, "Like Prince!" he'd exclaimed—lived in a modest home along the shore on the opposite side of town and hosted clients in his living room, which was decorated like something out of a high-end architectural magazine. A tall and gawky man of perhaps thirty-five, with meticulously styled hair and designer clothing, he looked better suited to the chic streets of Beverly Hills than a small and unassuming town like Blissful Point, and the moment Katherine met him she recognized having seen him around town from time to time over the years.

"Katherine," he said in an agreeable voice, "it's a pleasure to meet you."

She smiled and shook his hand. It was warm and smooth. "Nice to meet you too."

Marcy was right, she thought. There was nothing eerie about Jacques at all. He seemed anything but a fortune teller.

"Before we get started," he said, motioning to a plush sofa where Katherine and Marcy were to sit, "it's important that you be comfortable as possible. There's nothing to be afraid of. I'm not a devil worshiper or a crazy person. I earn my living in the graphic design industry. This, I do part-time. It's a gift from my spirit guides."

Katherine nodded and smiled, unsure of how else to respond. She sat on the couch. It was comfortable, and she relaxed, allowing the cushions to surround her.

"Let's get a few things out in the open," Jacques continued. "Blissful Point is a small town. Taking that—and the things I've discussed with Marcy during her sessions where you've come up—into consideration, I obviously know who you are to a degree already. I'm aware that you operate the cabins on the lake and that your husband James disappeared a little over a year ago. I also know about the little boy that drowned there. Other than that and some small incidental things that appeared in the newspaper when those events occurred, I know virtually nothing else about you personally. Clear?"

"Clear."

The room was dimly lit, only a small lamp on a table between them was on, but the room was more cozy and intimate than spooky. It was warm and welcoming here and radiated a feeling of tranquility and safety Katherine embraced.

"There's some white zin if you'd like some," Jacques said, nodding to three glasses of wine on the nearby coffee table. "It helps to relax."

Marcy scooped hers up but Katherine politely shook her head no.

Jacques smiled warmly. "It's there if you want it, okay?"

Outside, in the darkness, the snow had begun. Light flakes blew about, offering up the delicate sort of snow that often signaled the beginning of a blizzard. It always came first, this sparse and harmless-looking snow, and was almost always followed by much worse.

"I don't know if Marcy told you how I work, but I don't use cards or tea leaves or anything like that," Jacques explained. "What I like to do is to hold something of yours, or your husband's, if you want me to focus on him. I notice you wear a wedding ring."

Katherine glanced at her hand. She hadn't taken the gold band off even once in all the years she and James had been married. "Yes," she said uneasily. "I…still do."

"Would it be all right if I held it while we talk?"

She'd come close to removing it on more than one occasion since James's disappearance, but never had. "I don't know," she said awkwardly. "I'm sure this sounds silly but I haven't taken it off since the day he put it on my finger."

"No, it doesn't sound silly at all." Jacques gave a wide smile, revealing a set of perfectly white, capped teeth. "I only suggested it because a wedding ring, being such an intimate item, is often very effective. But you need to be comfortable, Katherine, that's paramount here."

Marcy elbowed her none too subtly and eyed the wedding ring.

"And *you*," he said playfully, pointing a finger at Marcy. "Behave."

Marcy flashed him an equally playful scowl, sat back deeper into the couch and sipped her wine. "I'm only trying to help."

Katherine gazed down at her ring awhile but said nothing.

"Let the thoughts, memories and feelings you're experiencing right now flow free."

The soothing sound of his voice broke her concentration.

"Let them come to you," Jacques said. "Let them wash over you like gentle waves."

Katherine twisted the ring and slowly pulled it up over her knuckle. "I guess…I guess it would be all right." She hesitated a moment, watching it there on her hand, then slid it off the end of her finger. A deep moat of smooth pale skin lay in its wake. Like a scar, she thought.

Jacques took her hand in both of his and gently allowed the ring to pass from her palm to his. With another warm smile, he leaned back a bit, letting her hands go, and moved the band slowly between his fingers, as if inspecting it for imperfections or divots. He drew a deep breath, held it a few seconds then released it in a long rush, his eyes closing as he did so. "Okay," he whispered to no one in particular. "Katherine, do you have any family?"

"No, my parents are both deceased, and I'm an only child."

"Strange." Jacques frowned but his eyes remained closed. His fingers moved over the ring. "I'm getting a strong sense of a group dynamic here, like you're part of a larger group. I normally only get this with twins or people from large and close families, or at a minimum, in someone with profoundly close sibling or parental ties."

Katherine glanced at Marcy. She gave her a look that said: *Be patient.*

"Your husband," he asked suddenly, "was he an only child as well?"

"James was an orphan. He never knew for sure if he had any brothers or sisters."

Jacques said nothing for a few moments. "I'm also getting strong feelings of isolation and loneliness. It's highly unusual to get feelings of duality like that so strongly in one person. Could be that the energy I'm picking up is originating from more than one source. It happens now and then."

"Is that bad?" Katherine asked.

"Not in the least." His eyes remained closed but moved beneath the lids rapidly. "I know this is an odd question, and please don't be offended, but has anyone else ever worn this ring?"

"No, of course not, why would—"

"Do you and James have children?"

"No." *This guy is awful*, she thought, *what am I doing here?*

"You're certain James never had children?"

"Yes, I'm certain," Katherine said in a tone that signaled annoyance had gotten the better of her. "He was my husband. We were married in our early twenties. If he'd had children in his teens, don't you think he might've mentioned it?"

"I mean no disrespect, Katherine." Jacques slowly opened his eyes. "I'm just telling you what I feel."

"No, actually you're asking me questions. So far you're zero-for-three."

Marcy sat up quickly. "Katherine, you have to—"

"Marcy, *please*," Jacques said without raising his voice. "It's all right, Katherine, express yourself honestly. The energy is pure and therefore—"

"Is my husband alive or dead?" Katherine asked suddenly.

His eyes remained locked on hers, but seemed to be looking right through her. He gave no indication that he'd taken her question as the challenge she'd intended it to be. "I'm getting a very odd sense of him, a very distant sense of him, and yet…it's hard to describe. Those who have passed over come through very differently than those still here. I don't say *'died'* because we don't die, we simply change. But right now I'm getting a strange mixture of the two, as if he's somehow near to both, straddling them maybe. It happens sometimes with people who are close to crossing but haven't yet."

"You mean people on their deathbeds?"

"That's one example, yes."

"Then he's still alive?"

"I—I'm honestly not certain." Jacques sighed, clearly frustrated. "If he's passed on, it was very recently. If he hasn't, and is still here, he isn't well and won't be much longer. He may be having trouble passing, it happens if the situation is less than…let's just say, 'pleasant'. Sometimes if there are unresolved issues where—"

"Then he's alive but—what—sick?"

"Yes, if he's still on this plane of existence. But I can't be certain he's still here."

"Is there anything you *can* be certain of?"

"God, Katherine," Marcy said, "stop being so negative already."

Jacques quieted her with another glance. "I apologize if I'm not giving specific enough answers for you, Katherine. I simply tell you what I feel and sense. Sometimes the process is a slow one, but it builds the longer we talk."

"I'm sorry, I—"

"Don't be, it's fine. You're nervous and you've been under a lot of stress for a long while now." Jacques waved a hand in the air as if to shoo the negativity away. "I have to tell you I'm getting a very strong sense of children. I'm sorry, but I can't shake it. It's coming through quite vividly."

Katherine stared at him, saying nothing.

"If this is too personal a question I'll understand, but—"

"No, I've never had an abortion," she said. "There were no children."

"There are children all around you, Katherine."

"I'm telling you there were no children."

His eyes slid shut. "And I'm telling *you*...there are."

"This is ridiculous, what does any of this have to do with—"

"Maybe they're not literal," he explained. "They could be representational of something else in your life, mind, heart or soul."

"Such as?"

"That's not quite clear to me." Jacques cleared his throat a few times like he was trying not to cough. "But the fear is. Your fear, you—you're afraid. It's a deep fear, the kind that goes straight through to your soul. It's almost childlike in its intensity."

Katherine felt a chill lick the back of her neck.

His fingers massaged the gold band. "You're...my God, you're *terrified*. But you...you're not entirely sure why, are you?"

"No," she said softly, "I'm not."

"I'm getting...water. Usually that's a positive thing. It tends to represent cleansing or rebirth. Of course, since you live on a lake it could simply mean that as well. But there's so much of it. I'm getting so much of it, so much so...so much it's like—like I'm drowning." He cleared his throat again, loudly this time. "It's the lake, isn't it? That's it. It's the lake you fear."

The chill left her, replaced by strange slowly spreading warmth. "Yes, I..." She glanced at Marcy, who stared back with anticipation. "Yes, I'm no longer comfortable around the lake, that's true."

"But you say you don't know why?"

"That's right."

He nodded, eyes still shut. "It's more than discomfort, though. It's fear. You fear the lake, you—you *hate* it."

"Yes."

"How have you stayed there with this level of fear? It's uncanny."

"It was bad for a long time before James disappeared," she told him. "He was on a steady decline and—"

"My *God*, there's darkness when you mention him. I can feel it moving through me and growing every time you say his name."

"He was ill," she said. "He was suffering, slowly losing his grip on reality."

"You believe..." Jacques slipped the wedding ring over the tip of his left index finger, and with his other hand gripped the band and slowly turned it. His eyes opened, found Katherine. "You think James is still there?"

She forced a swallow. She had never told anyone that before.

"You think he's still at the lake," Jacques said, no longer a question. "But not like before. Not...exactly."

"Yes," she said softly, her confrontational tone replaced with one more closely resembling discomfort. "I—well, I think he might be but—but only in a sense. I think it's possible that his memory lingers and—"

"No, that's not true." His expression shifted, like his head had just cleared. "You need to be honest with me. You think he's still there but...but that it's not really him. You think maybe it never was. You're questioning your entire life with him and—"

"You're wrong." Katherine caught hold of herself.

"Am I, Katherine?"

"We had many happy years together."

Jacques shook his head. "Such sorrow, it—it's so heavy. He...he hasn't crossed over yet, Katherine. It's clearer now, I—I don't think he's completely gone yet. He's running. James is running but he's not alone."

"James is dead," Katherine said flatly.

"We don't die. And if you believed we did, you wouldn't be here talking with me."

"I'd like my wedding ring back now, please." Katherine held her hand out. "I think it's time for me to go."

"He's not alone," Jacques said again.

"My ring, please, may I have it?"

"He's with the children."

Katherine stood up, her entire body shaking. "Give me my wedding band back."

"He's with the children, Katherine."

"There aren't any fucking children!"

Marcy scrambled to her feet, put her wine aside and reached out for Katherine. "It's okay, honey, take it easy."

Jacques held the ring out for her. "I'm sorry if I frightened you. Sometimes in the heat of the moment my concentration is such that I go into something similar to a trance."

Katherine snatched the ring but didn't put it back on her finger. Instead she dropped it into her purse. "This wasn't a good idea. I—I'm sorry, I don't mean to disrespect you in your own home but I—look, what do I owe you?"

"This isn't a carnival, Katherine."

"You do expect me to pay you, don't you?"

"I'd like to continue," he said. "I know this is difficult for you but I think it's important that we delve deeper here. I'm not interested in money. I'm trying to help you, and I'm getting some very intense—"

She removed a twenty from her wallet and placed it on the coffee table. "If that's not sufficient you can bill me."

"I'm truly sorry if I upset you."

"Thank you, I know it wasn't intentional." Katherine forced a smile. "I've made enough of a fool of myself tonight. Thanks for your time. Marcy, come on."

Marcy quickly gathered her things. "Sorry, Jacques, she gets emotional sometimes and—"

"Katherine?" he said, ignoring Marcy as he slowly rose from the couch.

She turned, looked back at him.

"These things won't simply go away. You need to face and resolve them if possible."

"Yes, I understand. Thank you for your time."

"You're planning to move from the lake," he said abruptly.

She nodded.

"It's a good plan. Do it as soon as possible. I'm getting a lot of negativity around it, a lot of dark energy that's very…unsettling. There's something more here than you know—more than I know and understand yet—something *extraordinary*. But just the same, it's not healthy for you there anymore."

"You mean it's not safe."

Jacques stared at her but offered no further elaboration.

The look in his eyes swept through her mind then slowly faded to memory, replaced by the spiraling flakes of the here and now just beyond the sliders.

The snow was getting heavier.

Katherine moved to the adjacent kitchen and grabbed the phone. No dial tone.

She went quickly to her bedroom and tried that extension, but it too was dead. It was not unusual for lines to be down during a snowstorm of this size, and when they did go down, it was usually hours before repair personnel arrived. In storms like this, she realized it might very well be days. Still, she couldn't help but feel it was too convenient to be coincidence. Although life in Blissful Point was quiet and lacked any violent crime rate to speak of, obviously it wasn't outside the realm of possibility that the stranger had cut her phone lines prior to his sudden arrival. Just because he had a child with him didn't grant him immunity from evil. Some criminals even used children as shields or decoys, as a means of obtaining trust from unsuspecting victims. She had read about such things.

There are children all around you, Katherine.

Katherine returned to the den, found her cell phone on an end table and flipped it open. No signal. "Of course," she muttered. "It just figures, doesn't it?"

She paced about the den, sipping her now lukewarm coffee and mumbling the maelstrom of possibilities clogging her mind. Barney had taken position along the back of a recliner in the corner, watching over the proceedings with keen but impassive eyes.

"You saw them too," she said, remembering the cat's growl upon the man's arrival. *But what else do you see?* she wondered. *What else do you know?*

Barney slowly closed his eyes then just as slowly slid them open again.

She thought of the little girl, so tiny and helpless, her face hidden in the hooded coat as the storm raged around her. Katherine knew firsthand how cold the winters were here, how the wind off the lake could cut through you like a razor. Guilt came to her in waves, bringing with it memories of the little Japanese boy, his small body limp and dead, dripping wet, swallowed then vomited up by the lake.

On foot and in these conditions, the man might last awhile but the little girl certainly would not. Surely they had a car, a vehicle of some kind, she told herself. Even if it had gone off the road, they could still take shelter in it and survive off the heater until the storm passed, weakened, or until someone passed by who might help, couldn't they? But if the car were dead, she knew neither of them would last long huddled in the husk of an automobile. Not in these temperatures.

She saw James crying and rocking the dead Japanese boy in his arms, the boy's diminutive limbs dangling and swaying lifelessly as his parents looked on. Their faces were burned into her consciousness like a brand, and though Katherine had learned to forget many things in her life, to set them aside and bury them or pretend they had never happened and to move on, as life often demanded, the faces of that young couple would never be among them.

With a reserved but devoted air, Barney watched her silently, as if he had read her mind and now awaited her decision.

Katherine put her coffee aside, and tried the cell phone again. The display read: *Searching for Signal.* She snapped the phone shut and went back to the bedroom.

Without stopping to think about it, she threw off her robe and caught a glimpse of her reflection in the freestanding full-length mirror in the corner. Startled, she stopped in her tracks like she'd never seen herself out of clothes. It was her ribs that first caught her attention. She'd lost a lot of weight in the past year, and they now hung beneath the surface of her skin, a fence of bone below her breasts, rising and falling with each nervous breath. Her stomach was so flat it appeared nearly hollow and sunken at certain angles, and her face seemed intrusive, her once soft features covered now with only a thin layer of skin stretched taut over severe slopes and pointed knolls. She turned slightly, rising up on the balls of her feet. She'd never been busty by any stretch of the imagination—a B cup since high school—but her breasts, though firm and nicely shaped, looked a bit smaller than they'd once been, and though they, like her legs and buttocks, appeared to belong to a woman younger than forty-five years, she noticed that her weight loss had caused similar illusions in the rest of her body as well, though most of them negative. She had been stronger in years past, more sinewy and substantial, but now appeared fragile, drawn, anxious and weak. Black rings circled her bloodshot eyes like a raccoon mask, and her lips were pale and chapped.

She brought a finger very slowly to her mouth, touched the rough and flaked skin there, as if to be certain she was in fact looking at herself.

God help me, she thought. Near the end James had looked this way too.

Katherine had never felt quite so vulnerable in all her life, and her nudity was only making it worse. She changed quickly into a pair of jeans, boots, a turtleneck and a heavy wool sweater, and by the time she was dressed she had convinced herself that at least attempting to drive into town would be best. The drive would allow her to use the payphone at the gas station to alert the phone company that her lines were down, and she could swing by the police station and tell them about the strange man and little girl.

Rather than look at her own reflection now, she focused on that of the bedroom floor behind her, and remembered how she had found James huddled there one early evening, his journal clutched to his chest as he sat on the floor, muttering under his breath, carrying on a conversation with no one, but animated and nodding in a way that suggested he believed there were others in the room with him. As always, his face was drawn and terror-stricken, but in this instance, he looked a bit more in control of himself, as if he were bartering, negotiating for his sanity. He had whirled around upon realizing she was in the doorway, looking like a child caught in the middle of something no parent would ever approve of.

Don't come in, he'd said, voice shaking. *Don't come in here, I—you can't come in here right now.*

James, please, she'd pleaded. *I can't do this anymore. You have to get help. You have to let me get you some help.*

James shook his head. *There is no help.*

She spent most nights on the couch now, as she hadn't been wholly comfortable in this room since.

The memory of Jacques's voice came to her. *It's not healthy for you there anymore.*

Katherine forced herself from the mirror but hesitated at the bedroom closet, where something other than memories had caught her attention. She crouched and focused on a shotgun propped in the back corner. The gun had belonged to James. She'd only fired it twice, when years earlier he had insisted she learn the basics of the weapon just in case. He'd often seemed even more uncomfortable with it than she was, and she could never imagine either of them shooting anything, but it had been purchased as a precaution, a potentially necessary evil. *The winters here can be desolate,* he'd once said, *you just never know today.*

The recollection of the man with black eyes flashed through her mind. What if he was waiting out there somewhere for her? What if by cutting the phone lines he knew she would eventually venture outside to her Bronco and go for help? She'd be walking right into his trap. The entire scenario sounded ludicrous, but the fear and uncertainty was suffocating and anything but imagined.

There is no help.

Heart racing, Katherine grabbed the shotgun, a box of shells, and headed for the door.

CHAPTER SIX

Carlo began the morning the way he began most mornings: hung over and feeling vaguely guilty about it. Normally his sleep was drunken, dreamless and deep, but now and then he still dreamed. They were rarely pleasant dreams, however, and that night had been no exception. He'd dreamt of James, Katherine and the lake— of that much he was certain—but he couldn't seem to recall any specific details. All he could remember was a horrible sense of terror and pain associated with the dream, but otherwise it was vague and formless.

He glanced around the apartment at the empty whiskey bottles and sighed. The dream wasn't the only thing he couldn't remember clearly. The empty bottles indicated he'd downed them all, but much of the evening prior was a blur.

Today's going to be different, he told himself. Of course he made that promise to himself nearly every day, but on this one he was determined to live up to it by doing something good, something positive. He'd do something to help Katherine even if she hadn't exactly gone ahead and given her blessing for him to do so, and in the end she would see that he was doing what was best, looking into things for her and being useful. Carlo hadn't felt that way in a very long time.

Something drew him to his bookcase. Amidst the endless paperbacks and occasional hardcover, he kept a photo album he'd compiled while in college. It chronicled those years wonderfully, and mostly contained photos of parties and dorm rooms, women he'd dated and some he'd only wanted to, friends and lovers, and of course, various pictures of him and Katherine.

Though they meant a great deal to him, Carlo often found walks down memory lane too painful to endure, so he rarely looked at them. In fact, he hadn't gone through the album in as long as he could remember, and while something told him today was probably not the best time to start reminiscing, he felt inexplicably compelled to look at the old photographs.

Carlo crouched next to the shelf that held the album. It looked odd to him, out of place or not quite right somehow. There was no doubt this was his photo album—he only had the one—but it looked too new. He remembered the exterior as older and somewhat worn. "Weird," he said through a yawn. Pulling the album free, he rubbed his eyes, did his best to focus then flipped it open.

With brows knit, he suddenly felt his heart drop then just as suddenly race to the point where he found it difficult to draw a deep breath.

The pages were empty.

He flipped through page after page, turning them more and more frantically with each try, until he'd reached the end. Nothing, not one photograph, no trace of them or any indication that the album had ever held even a single photograph. But how could that be? How could they all be gone?

Although he knew it was ridiculous, Carlo inspected the empty space on the bookshelf to see if the photographs had all somehow fallen out. When that turned up nothing, he again examined the album. It looked like the same one he'd had for years, but it couldn't be. He distinctly remembered the wear on the other one.

"Then where the hell did this come from?" he mumbled. "And where's my old one?"

Carlo tried to remember if he'd purchased a second album at some point and simply forgotten. Still, even if that were the case, he knew he'd never get rid of the original. Those photographs meant too much to him.

He tossed the empty album aside and rummaged through the bookcase, pulling books free until the shelves were bare.

Could he have thrown it out or misplaced it during one of his drunken binges? he wondered. Could he have done such a thing and have no memory of it whatsoever? It just didn't seem possible to him. The booze regularly affected his memory, but he found it hard to believe he could forget destroying something so important to him.

Confusion and fear gave way to depression and self-loathing.

"Way to go, fuck-up," he said, telling himself he had to be responsible for the missing photographs. He must have done something to them while drunk. What other explanation could there possibly be? Carlo looked down at the open album lying at his feet.

Bare, plastic-covered pages stared back.

It was like his very past was gone, stolen from him in his sleep.

Or like it had never really existed in the first place.

After a lengthy shower, he drove from his apartment to the outskirts of town, taking back roads to a desolate stretch of land that led to a tavern set back from the road.

The lot was empty, but for one unmarked police car and a motorcycle. Neon beer signs buzzed in the dark windows. The snow had begun the night before, but things were going to get far worse, according to the weather reports.

As Carlo entered the bar, it took a moment for his eyes to adjust to the dimly lit room. He focused and saw Reggie sitting in a booth against the far wall. He looked out of place and stiff, unmistakably a cop.

"How's it going?" a rotund bartender said.

Carlo brushed some snow from his jacket. "Good, man, how you doing?"

"Can I get you something?"

"Just a black coffee when you get a chance." Carlo pointed to the booth where Reggie was sitting, then headed toward it. "I'll be over there."

He'd not yet reached the booth when Reggie rose to his feet and extended a hand. He was still an intimidating physical presence. "Carlo Damone," Reggie said through a bright white smile. "The man. The legend."

"In the flesh, baby." Carlo threw his hand out and watched it disappear into Reggie's enormous mitt. "What's happening, Reg?"

"Same ole," he said. "You don't look so good, Damone."

Carlo slid into the booth and sat down. "I don't feel so good."

"Nice place," he said with sarcasm so thick it could've qualified as fog. "Not exactly a family place. A restaurant would've worked, maybe a coffee shop."

"It's cool. They have good coffee here and a decent grill. Good breakfasts."

"I probably shouldn't be hanging out in a place where it looks like they sell crack out of the men's room, know what I mean?"

The bartender appeared with Carlo's coffee, placed it in front of him. "I figured we'd have some privacy here, that's all," he said once the bartender had left. "Jesus, relax, it's just a bar and grill, man."

"You don't have business here by any chance?" Reggie asked.

Carlo felt his stomach sink. Some ghosts never ceased to haunt. "What the fuck is that supposed to mean?"

"You know what it means."

"Jesus, I don't see you in all this time and you hit me with that shit?"

"Have to ask, man, I'm sorry."

"I dealt drugs in *school*, for Christ's sake."

"Look, I don't know what your life is now, okay? I'm sorry to be a prick but I can't just do whatever the hell I want anymore."

He hadn't seen Reggie in years, literally once or twice since their college days, and now this was the second time he'd spoken to him in less than a week. The first had been a simple call placed to his home in Boston, a brief conversation followed by a request for a favor and some information. This time when Carlo had called to find out what his friend had for him, Reggie suggested they meet face-to-face.

"You're the one that wanted to meet," Carlo reminded him. "I was willing to do this by phone. If you were worried about tarnishing your reputation, then you should've—"

"I thought it'd be nice to see you, all right?"

"Then why are you being such a dildo?"

Reggie locked the fingers of both hands together then cracked his knuckles with a loud *snap-pop*. After a moment of awkward silence, his posture relaxed somewhat and he offered a nod. "It's not like it was before, that's all I'm saying. I have to be careful about who I associate with and where I go."

"You still do drugs, Reg?"

"Of course not, I'm a fucking police officer, what's wrong with you?"

"Just wondering because, you know, in college you were one of my best customers." He held his chin with his hand. "Wait, come to think of it, so were some of the cops in town."

The big man's jaw clenched. "College was a long time ago, Damone."

Carlo calmly sipped his coffee. "Yeah, sure was."

The muscles in Reggie's face gradually softened. "Point taken."

"We're all just trying to make it through the day, man. Okay?"

"Okay." Reggie nodded knowingly. "No hard feelings, all right?"

"No hard feelings." Carlo raised his mug and Reggie lifted his own in response. He was back to playing it light, but Carlo could tell he was still uncomfortable.

"Seriously, it's good to see you, Damone."

"It's good to be seen." Carlo mustered a smile. His old friend was as powerfully built as ever, still in great shape and impressive in a black pinstripe suit. His hair was trimmed short and neat in a military-style cut, and a pencil-thin mustache added a nice touch to his overall appearance. On his left hand he sported a shiny gold wedding band that contrasted nicely with his dark skin. "How's Debbie doing, you know, besides having to put up with you?"

"She's fine," Reggie chuckled.

"And the kids?"

"Daniel's a junior over at Bridgewater State College, and Sarah's engaged. Wedding's scheduled for next summer."

"God we're old."

"Nah, just all grown up."

As another uncomfortable silence fell over the booth, Carlo took the opportunity to study Reggie a bit more closely. He looked as rested and healthy as any forty-five-year-old Massachusetts State Police Investigator had a right to. He seemed frozen at about thirty or so, like he'd barely aged at all since then. "Listen, I know you're busy," Carlo eventually said, "and I appreciate you taking the time to do this for me."

"Happy to do what I can."

"I told Kate I'd try to get whatever information on James I could get my hands on, and figured with your connections you could get some background on him that maybe we couldn't."

"She could've contacted me herself, I would've—"

"Like I told you on the phone, this whole thing's embarrassing for her."

"We're all old friends, no reason to be embarrassed." Reggie's eyes brightened a bit. "I was glad to hear you guys are still close. Katherine was always a good friend to you, helped keep your sorry ass in line."

"Yeah, well we all got our crosses to bear." Carlo smirked. "During that whole mess out at the lake, did you see her at all?"

"We briefly investigated the disappearance of her husband but it was ultimately a local matter. I wasn't involved personally. I was in the middle of another case at the time, but I heard about it like everybody else. It was all over the news for a while. I felt bad. I should've called or sent Katherine a note or something."

"We've all got a few should-haves laying around, man."

He shrugged his broad shoulders. "From everything I heard it looked like her husband just up and walked out on her one night. Damn shame, but unfortunately that kind of thing happens all the time."

Before another lull could set in, Carlo asked, "So what'd you find?"

"To be honest, not much, but I'll give you what I got." Reggie's eyes shifted and locked back on him. "On the drowning death of the kid, I talked to a couple of the local people involved in the investigation. Everybody agreed the kid just fell, hit his head and drowned. Even the coroner felt it was an accident."

"But they could've been wrong, right?"

"You think they were?"

"I don't know, I'm just asking, they could've been wrong, right?"

"Is it possible? Of course, but I'd say unlikely."

"What about the background stuff?"

"If you had your hopes up for some big revelation, you're gonna be disappointed. There wasn't much to get, but I got some notes." He retrieved a small notebook from a briefcase on the seat next to him. "Seems your boy was a Doe Baby."

"What the hell is that?"

"You know, like a John or a Jane Doe, only an infant," he said, flipping open the notebook. "A priest found him in a church in some backwoods town up in the western part of the state, apparently abandoned by his birth mother. It happens. They usually find something to tie the baby to someone—not always but usually—but in this case they never did."

"Jesus, so even James had no idea who he was."

"Sad, I know, but like I said, it happens. You knew James, right?"

"A little bit."

"I didn't get a lot of specifics, but I guess he lived with a few foster families—you know, bouncing around like a lot of those poor kids do—until he was nine. At that point he ended up with a couple named Darren and Josephine Covington, where he remained until legal adulthood."

"Yeah, I knew that already." Carlo took another swallow of coffee. "What else you got?"

"From what little I came across the guy led a very average and uneventful life. Middle of the road all the way, no great accomplishments but no real trouble either. No criminal record, I can tell you that. I don't think this guy ever even had so much as a speeding ticket." Reggie flipped to another page in his notebook. "Got some education info—where he went to high school and college—and some basic employment info, but most of it is very dated, and again, nothing stands out. Plus, where he and Katherine bought that lake property in their twenties he was self-employed for most of his life and that limits the amount of records there are."

"Anything else?"

Reggie looked at him over the top of his notebook. "Look, the bottom line is that from all indications, James lived a really unremarkable life. At least until he disappeared anyway."

Carlo finished his drink. "You think he's dead?"

"I got no idea."

"What about the guys that investigated it, what do they think?"

"That he probably got tired of his old lady and took a walk. Only thing is, he didn't take anything with him, and that is unusual. It's probably the only reason they went to the extent they did, dragging the lake and all that. He didn't take any credit cards with him, no clothes, money, nothing—just the clothes on his back and supposedly some journal. And there's been no trace of him since. But it's a big world out there, Damone, and people disappear every day, so many that when you see the statistics it boggles the mind. But a lot of them just walk away from their lives, and that's probably the case with this guy too."

"Just doesn't add up to me," Carlo said.

"These kinds of things rarely do. The problem is that a lot of these people who vanish don't want be found. And trust me, once you disappear into the wild blue yonder, it's not that hard to stay gone."

Carlo nodded wearily. "Thanks for taking the time to do this, I appreciate it. I was hoping maybe you'd come up with something I could run with, maybe help Katherine figure all this out, you know?"

"I wish I had something that helped, but this guy was clean. So clean it's almost a little suspicious to be honest, but clean nonetheless. And I know I don't have to tell you this but no one at any point—except for initially when you have to at least consider the possibility—ever had any suspicions when it came to Katherine. They interviewed her a couple times, fairly extensively, and nobody believes there was foul play of any kind, and that even if there eventually was, it occurred after his disappearance and that Katherine had nothing to do with it."

Carlo looked down into his coffee. "Just out of curiosity, did you get anything on the foster parents?"

"Not much," he said, referring again to his notebook. "I didn't really look into the Covingtons because you said you wanted background on James. If you wanted information on them you should've said so, I could've—"

"It's cool, just wondered if you got anything basic on them, like a location maybe."

Reggie consulted his notes. "All I got on them was that the husband's deceased. The wife, Josephine Covington, has a listed residence in Littlebrook, Rhode Island. But that's it. I'm not even sure she still lives there or if she's even alive at all for that matter, the info was a couple years old. I could've found out more on them but like I said, man, if you wanted background on them you should've—"

"You got an actual address for Josephine Covington?"

He tore a sheet from his notebook, and with his pen transferred the information to it. "You think she might know something?" he asked, sliding it across the table.

"Probably not, but it might be worth a shot talking to her."

Once again Reggie looked uncomfortable, like the booth was too small to properly accommodate him, which it probably was. He seemed to think about his response for a while before offering it. "I don't see what good it'll do, far as I can tell James had no traffic with these people since he was a kid, and if the date of birth I got on her is right, Josephine Covington's in her eighties, probably doesn't remember what she had for breakfast yesterday never mind some foster kid she had almost thirty years ago. But if you want I'll see what I can come up with on her for you."

"Don't worry about it, but thanks. I'll go back and talk to Katherine, let her know you were able to locate Josephine. Maybe she'll want to talk to her herself."

Reggie folded his notebook closed and put it back into the briefcase on the seat. "Hope it all works out for her. Tell her I said hello, all right?"

"I will."

"I better get going."

"Stick around and have some breakfast, we'll catch up on—"

"Can't, got to get to work. Besides, that storm's coming in fast. It's already getting bad." Reggie offered his hand. "It was good seeing you, Damone."

Now that their business was concluded it was obvious Reggie couldn't get out of there fast enough. He'd done this because he'd felt he had to, not because he'd wanted to. Carlo understood. He was only a phantom to Reggie now, a relic from some jaded past he preferred to forget, an odd piece that no longer fit the puzzle. Carlo was used to it. He hadn't been useful or even entertaining to those from his earlier days in some time. To those like Reggie he was a disposable memory better left in the past where he belonged, a character referred to in old college stories at parties, good for a laugh and a fond or even embarrassing reminiscence but not much else. In the real world he was a reminder of how not everyone makes it out in one piece. Some get left behind.

Carlo shook his hand and smiled anyway. "Yeah, man, you too."

CHAPTER SEVEN

K atherine watched the deck and property beyond for several minutes. Another swell of guilt hit as she again pictured the little girl out in the storm, collapsed or shivering somewhere nearby, the snow covering her, concealing her, ingesting her small body into the landscape. Dead. She saw the little girl dead among the trees, frozen like some demonic sculpture, grisly and hopeless.

Don't be so dramatic, she told herself.

But Katherine knew all too well that since the drowning death of the Japanese boy, she could no longer see or think of children without also thinking of death. Even in the most mundane circumstances—passing them on the street, seeing them frolic on a playground or having dinner at a restaurant—their innocent faces always turned to death masks.

It hadn't always been like that—she'd once loved to interact with and watch children at play while visiting the lake—though for most of her adult life the subject of children, generally speaking, had been a sore one. Early in their relationship, she and James had decided against having children, not because they disliked them, simply because they preferred instead a life of freedom and time together. But neither quite realized the extent to which they would be forced to defend that decision over the years, and how it would open them to frequent ridicule. In the minds of many, a woman with no desire to give birth was heretical and somehow blaspheming against God and nature, as if the path to becoming a worthy and complete human being could only be found through reproduction.

James had shared her feelings on the subject, agreeing that children would complicate their lives and change things to a degree he was not comfortable with. He was happy with her, their cat Barney, the lake, their home and his writing. He was content, and together, they were whole. Once, not so very long ago, they had been whole.

"It's true," she said, converting her thoughts to audible words as she had when James was still in the house with her, by her side and able to hear them. "Weren't we whole once, James, the two of us, not so very long ago?"

The wind blew snow against the sliders in answer. Katherine moved closer, eyes sweeping the property, shotgun in hand. *How ridiculous I must look*, she thought. *What an absurd ass I've become, standing here with this old gun watching the falling snow; frightened of a lost man and his young daughter and every other goddamn thing in the world and in my head.*

Katherine refocused her attention on the property, and once satisfied that the man was neither lurking nearby nor waiting for her at some point between the slider door and her vehicle, she fumbled keys from her purse and stepped outside.

She hadn't any idea just how cold it was. Closing the slider behind her and tucking chin to chest, she scanned the area while moving quickly down the deck steps. As she crossed the small section of yard to her Bronco, she looked over at the rows of cabins. Dark and draped in fresh snow, they sat quietly amidst the still forest. Sprinkled about an otherwise pristine vista, they seemed more neglected and in an even greater state of disrepair than normal.

The remnants of a path that wound its way up into the surrounding forest caught her attention, the snow not quite as deep there yet, the shape of the path still visible, though barely, through the storm. She remembered the last time she and James had walked that path, hand in hand early one evening after dinner. Though both had crossed into their forties, he'd felt strong as he had in his twenties, she thought, his body still trim and sinewy, his gait vibrant. Before the madness only Katherine had begun to question her vitality, never James. *Think old and you become old*, he'd told her. *My God, Kate, we're only in our early forties, we're still kids!* To James, time had always been irrelevant, age a boundary strictly psychological in nature. *It's all in your mind, kiddo.*

Ironic, she thought. Perhaps he'd been right all along.

With the heavy shotgun held awkwardly down against her side, she turned away from the path and glanced again about the grounds. The man and little girl were nowhere in sight.

Moving quickly as she could in the snow, she reached the Bronco and pulled open the driver-side door. It gave a loud squeaking moan that echoed across the lot as she hopped up and slid inside the cab.

The steering wheel was freezing even through her knit gloves, and both the windshield and back window were coated with a thin film of ice. Thankfully, the engine turned over immediately, so she flipped on the defrosters and hugged herself a moment, her view obscured by vaporous breath.

Through clouds of mist and icy portals along the windows, she watched the area as best she could; shifting her head from side to side in an attempt to see as much as possible. The man could be anywhere, and unless she saw him coming, he could easily creep up on her undetected. Being inside the cab produced a sudden and eerie sensation. Like being entombed, she imagined, here in this cold little open space, sealed off from the outside world yet still able to feel it. Odd, how being inside something as unexceptional as a car or truck gave a false sense of safety—separation from the rest of the world—as if once within its confines one became invisible. Like watching life from some other place, she thought, some separate place.

Yes, James whispered to her. *Yes.*

Though the heat filling the cab had taken the edge off the initial chill, another wave of cold hit her. She shuddered violently, but once it passed she dropped the Bronco into Drive and stepped on the gas. The tires whined, sliding against the ice beneath them. The Bronco rocked then lurched but didn't move. "Sonofabitch," she muttered. The windshield wipers squeaked with each pass, doing little to increase visibility through the swirl of thick flakes. She watched the heavily wooded road through the seemingly endless ocean of stark white, but saw no signs of life. But for the sound of the engine, the landscape was deathly silent.

After a few more attempts she realized the Bronco was hopelessly stuck. Without someone to help her push she'd never get it moving.

Katherine threw open the door, jumped down from the truck with the shotgun in tow and crossed back to the base of the deck steps.

An uneasy feeling of being watched swept through her.

She looked back over her shoulder and watched the forest a

moment.

Ignoring the icy spikes tickling her cheeks, she turned and started up the steps when something on the perimeter of her peripheral vision caught her attention.

Light.

The windows of the first cabin, the one closest to her house, were filled with soft yellow light. She dropped back down off the first step and started hesitantly toward the cabin. The door was ajar, but—how could that be possible? They were padlocked shut once the summer season ended and the electricity for the cabins had been shut off months prior. Yet from all appearances, the door had not been damaged, and what was coming from within was most certainly light.

He's here with us, watching us even though we can't see him, James had told her. *He's all around us and yet I...I've never felt so alone. Why, Katherine? Why do I feel so alone?*

She recalled an old painting she'd once seen in a book featuring fourteenth century art, a darkly conceived vision of a sickly thin man being led toward the open mouth of Hell by a great number of hideous winged demons. The name of the artist escaped her, but what had always struck her about the piece was the expression on the man's face. Even all these years later she could remember it with startling clarity, because rather than terror or sorrow, the artist had made an intriguing choice and instead given his doomed soul a look of abject loneliness. In the midst of all that evil and darkness, hand in hand with a brood of horrible and frightening creatures, the man was anything but alone, and yet Katherine had never seen anyone so utterly solitary in all her life. At least not until the day James had expressed the same feelings. He'd looked like the face in the painting, surrounded by his demons yet completely, hopelessly alone.

But he had not been alone. There *were* others among them; just as he'd told her.

She knew that now.

Heart pounding, Katherine clutched the shotgun tight and glanced at the ground between herself and the cabin. Crouching, she squinted through the spinning snow at a quickly fading set of tracks, and as her mind searched for answers, in one panicked motion, she stood up and looked back at the house.

It appeared just as she'd left it.

Katherine stood frozen in place, chest heaving, mind racing.

"Hello, Katherine."

CHAPTER EIGHT

By late morning the storm was already hitting southeastern Massachusetts fairly heavily, but in nearby Rhode Island the tiny flakes had begun less than an hour before. As Carlo crossed the state line he looked to the sky. He still had time to check out the Josephine Covington angle then get back home and hunker down before things got too out of control. "I hope," he sighed.

He grabbed his cell phone and dialed Katherine's number, but changed his mind and hung up before it connected. There was a good chance she might be upset with him for taking it upon himself to do this. The wiser choice, it seemed, was to wait and see what the meeting with the old woman yielded. If he was able to garner some important or useful information he'd phone Katherine right away.

Within half an hour he'd located the town of Littlebrook and the street address Reggie had given him as Josephine Covington's last known residence. The area was very rural and seemed sparsely populated even by Rhode Island standards, and was one of those quiet little towns that looked like it had been frozen in time since the late 1950s.

Carlo turned onto a side road bookended by two enormous but empty fields, and followed it for a few hundred yards until the silhouette of a house came into view.

The home Josephine Covington had apparently moved into not long after the death of her husband was surprisingly old and rundown. Clearly neglected, it sat like a giant forgotten monument to another era. The two-story, unimaginatively designed box-like structure was in desperate need of a paintjob, the old clapboard flaked and decomposing, the yard dead and mostly clumps of brown grass. Alone at the end of a desolate dirt road and set back on a large lot, the area looked unfinished, like the neighborhood that should have sprouted up around it years before had never materialized, leaving a lonely old house and the lonely old woman who occupied it.

Not far from the front steps, Carlo parked, and through the light snow, saw something moving. He squinted, watched the slowly gliding figure. As the windshield wipers made another pass, he realized he was looking at an old woman sitting on a porch swing, swaying back and forth in the breeze and seemingly oblivious to the snow.

"You have *got* to be shitting me," he mumbled, stepping from the car.

Had it not been for her presence, he might have assumed the house abandoned long ago. Now the entire scene looked like something out of some surreal Bergman film.

The porch swing rocked slowly, the rusty chains squeaking and squealing with each pass. The woman appeared to be looking directly at him but gave no indication that she'd actually seen him. She was astonishingly elderly, her face so severely wrinkled it resembled splintered and cracked clay. Her white hair was thin and too long for a woman of her years, and hung about either side of her gaunt face like worn curtains. In a light housedress and slippers, she should've been freezing, but instead appeared impossibly fragile and unaware, a skeleton with an ashen complexion dressed and posed there as if without her knowledge.

Carlo approached the woman slowly, unsure of what her reaction might be. She bowed her head, and he could not be sure if the woman had perhaps fallen asleep or simply hadn't yet seen him. As he crossed what remained of the front yard and cautiously climbed the steps to the porch, the woman again slowly raised her head.

Never before had he seen the ravages of age so evident in a person's face. Her mouth seemed frozen in a perpetual frown, and her eyes were covered in thick white cataracts. In her bony, arthritically mangled hands were a set of wooden rosary beads, a gold crucifix dangling from the last length of beads swaying in time with the temperate motion of the porch swing.

"Mrs. Covington?"

The woman stared at him with eyes that saw nothing.

"Ma'am, are you Josephine Covington?"

She nodded slowly and with great effort, milky eyes looking right through him.

"Mrs. Covington, you—you don't know me, my name's Carlo Damone. I'm a close friend of Katherine's."

The woman offered no reply.

"James's wife, *Katherine*," he said, this time more emphatically. "I was hoping to talk with you about James, ma'am. Your son, James, Mrs. Covington, he's missing. A little over a year ago he disappeared without a trace. Were you aware of this?"

Her lips moved soundlessly in prayer, the wooden beads slowly sliding between her gnarled fingers.

"Mrs. Covington, do you understand? I've driven quite a distance to see you, this is very important. Have you seen James? Have you heard from him? He's gone missing. Your son, James, Mrs. Covington, he's missing."

This time the word *son* seemed to register, and her head moved sluggishly to the side, as if she had heard something farther in the distance and was straining to make it out. "My son," she said in a weak and raspy voice.

"Yes, your son." Carlo looked around. Could this woman possibly still live here unattended? She seemed just barely coherent and physically incapable of caring for herself. "Are you alone here, Mrs. Covington? Does someone look after you? Would you like to go inside, it's awfully cold out and it's snowing, you really need to be inside, don't you—"

"My son died," she said softly.

"No, we—we don't know that James has died, he's missing, he—"

"Parker," the woman said suddenly, and with more strength than she appeared to have.

"Pardon?"

"Parker. My son."

Katherine hadn't mentioned James having a foster brother, but it was certainly possible that he had. "I don't understand, Mrs. Covington, was Parker another foster child of yours?"

"Why would you ask for him now, after all this time? He was just a little boy, my—my poor, precious, beautiful little boy. He was my *child*."

Carlo could only surmise that Josephine and her husband had

had another child, a son named Parker who had evidently died years before. Perhaps this explained why they decided to bring a foster child like James into their lives, and he suspected it also more than likely explained why they had struck Katherine as so emotionally cold and detached. "Mrs. Covington, do you remember Katherine?"

The old woman nodded wearily. "Katherine."

"Yes. Katherine. Your son James married her, do you remember? I'm a friend of—"

"James wasn't our son."

"Foster son," he corrected himself.

"Parker was our son."

"Have you heard from James? He's missing, Mrs. Covington, do you understand?"

The steady squeak of the porch swing was the only response. Frustrated, Carlo nodded, even though he was relatively certain the woman was completely blind. He slowly backed away down the porch steps. Josephine Covington was clearly suffering from senility, among other afflictions, and the sky was turning an odd gray. The snow was getting worse, and he had a long drive home. "I'm sorry to have bothered you. Are you sure you're all right here all alone? I could call someone or..."

Discouraged by the silence that answered, Carlo turned and started for his car.

"He drowned, you know."

Carlo froze.

"Our son Parker, he drowned. Everyone thought it was an accident, even my damn fool husband. Until the day he died he believed Parker's death was an accident. He wanted to believe that, needed to. He believed it because James wanted him to. But you can't fool a mother. A mother knows certain things when it comes to her children. Gods should never take a child from their mother once it's given him or her to you. And if a god does, for no reason other than sport or vengeance, then it tells you just what kind of god he is, doesn't it? Ours is a merciful god, but not always a compassionate one. But then, our god isn't the only god, is he? There's a greater god even than him. This is what I've heard. I don't know if it's true...do you know if it's true?"

Carlo forced himself to look back over his shoulder. She stared back with blank eyes.

"I hope it is," she said. "When it happened again, the drowning of that little Japanese boy up at their lake, I—I told my husband, 'Do you see, Darren? Do you see?' He still didn't believe. But I know James. I know his secrets."

"What secrets, Mrs. Covington?" Carlo turned and took a few steps back toward the house, heart racing. "Can you tell those secrets to me?"

"I know his secrets because he told them to me."

"Please tell me what you know, ma'am."

"I had a terrible time with his delivery...almost died. He was special, our Parker, our special, precious boy. I couldn't have another, but we thought he needed an older brother, our little Parker."

James had not come after Parker then. He'd been there at the same time. They'd all been together, a family, until—

"I know what he did," Josephine Covington said. "I know what James did."

"What did James do, Mrs. Covington?"

"I've always known. I've always known what he did because he told me. Sometimes God tells you things too, things we think we want to know. But there are some things we should never know, things we're not meant to know. Not ever." The milky eyes glistened. Perhaps she saw and remembered far more than Carlo had initially suspected. "I know what James is, I've known for some time now."

"Where is he?"

"The water," she said, slurring her words like someone who had suffered a stroke. "Water teems with life. It—it's alive, did you know that? It heals and cleanses, but also kills. Did you know a great deal of the human body consists of water?"

"Yes ma'am."

"You don't see it, but it's there. Moving, flowing, alive within us and yet all we see is the exterior, a shell. It's not real, what we see, what he'll show you, what James will show you there—none of it's real. Just like the lake itself, there is the surface, and there is what lies beneath."

"They dragged the lake," he told her. "His body wasn't there."

"The lake," she said again. "James and the lake are the same."

"Has he gone back, is that it? Mrs. Covington, has James gone back to the lake?"

"He never left. He never will. Neither will Katherine." Her mouth drooped into a deeper frown, the heavy lines in her face growing worse. "And neither will you."

CHAPTER NINE

Katherine's heart leapt into the base of her throat as she whirled around in the direction of the voice. The door to the cabin had gone from ajar to fully open, and the interior of the cabin was filled with subtle light provided by a series of small candles positioned about the room. Katherine remembered how James had filled his small office in the house with candlelight from time to time. Many nights she had found him there, asleep at his keyboard or slumped over his journal, surrounded by slowly dying candles.

Melted wax had haunted her dreams ever since. Visions of James standing over her while she slept—a slowly burning candle clutched in his hands, the hot wax dripping over and burning her skin—had become a nightmare staple since his disappearance.

You're hurting me, James.

I would never hurt you, Katherine.

It burns, the pain is—

The pain sets you free, my love. It's what makes you alive.

With a subtle tilt of his hand, the wax dripped free, summoning her screams as James leaned closer, his face twisted into an expression of confusion and desperation. He raised the candle higher, and the wax began to drip across her face, scalding first her chin, then her mouth, cheeks and nose.

Not my eyes!

And then her eyes too were burned shut in darkness, the wax splashing and hardening over her lids.

A new skin, Katherine. Rebirth, do you understand?

Her muffled cries for help and a painful tightness in her chest made breathing nearly impossible, until she came awake each time with a start, gasping for breath and feeling her eyes to make sure they were still intact, a scream strangled deep in her throat.

Katherine blinked and pawed furiously at her eyes. Not wax, only snow, only snow.

She brushed the flakes from her face with her free hand, sweeping the dream memories away with them, and clutched the shotgun tighter with the other.

There was still no sign of the man, the little girl or anyone else, but someone had called her name, she was sure of it.

With the shotgun now held in both hands, she moved toward the cabin. Behind her, the wind grew stronger, blowing the powder about more violently and cutting through the nearby trees.

Just steps from the doorway she called out. "Hello?" Shadows moved beyond the threshold but no answer came. "Hello!" she called again. "Whoever's in there, I want you out here right now! You're trespassing! I have a gun!"

When again no response came, Katherine forced herself to cross the threshold and step into the cabin.

The stranger stood in the corner, watching her. Sitting on the edge of an old stripped down bed against the far wall was the little girl. Sans jacket, she was clad in a crimson velvet dress with white lace that seemed oddly formal under the circumstances. Golden hair hung to her narrow shoulders and her fair skin was tinted flush from the cold. Her eyes were gray and obviously sightless, yet they were trained directly on Katherine.

Unable to look away from the child, Katherine struggled to control her fear. "Why didn't you tell me she was…that she… Are you all right, sweetheart?"

The little girl's pale lips formed a grin.

With the shotgun shaking in her hands, Katherine eyed the man with increased confusion and stepped back a bit, closer to the storm. "Who are you people?"

The man, still in the corner, simply bowed his head.

"How did you get in here?" she demanded.

The man's eyes slid shut and his chest moved with a shallow rhythm indicative of sleep.

"Where's your mother?" Katherine asked the girl.

The child cocked her head like a baffled puppy, and in a tiny voice said, "Mother?"

"Yes, your—your mother, where is she?"

She grinned again, her bleak eyes staring and seeing nothing, yet burrowing straight through to whatever scraps of soul Katherine still possessed.

"Do you know where your mother is?"

The little girl's grin slowly faded. "James."

Her husband's name hung in the air between them like a foul odor.

The cold racked her so violently Katherine's upper body convulsed and she nearly dropped the weapon. "What did—what did you say?"

"*James.*"

Katherine felt herself slowly backing away from the child. "You know my husband?"

"James is our mother."

A burst of laughter escaped her before she could stop it. The sensation that she was cracking—shattering from the inside out—tore through her. "What did you—what are you talking about?"

"James is our mother."

"Stop saying that!" Katherine's body continued to quake with swells of terror and cold. "James is no one's *mother!*"

Confusion creased the little girl's face; a frown that indicated focused thought, but after a few seconds her expression revealed she had found the answer she'd so clearly been searching for. "Our father then?"

"What the hell are you talking about?" Katherine swung the shotgun around and aimed it at the man in the corner. "What is she talking about?"

In time with her trembling, the man's body began to shudder violently, and an odd splitting, squishing sound emanated from somewhere within his thrashing frame. Water, perhaps melted snow, formed a small pool around his feet.

"Don't be afraid," the little girl said, indicating the man as her vacant eyes blinked slowly. "You'll understand soon."

"What's happening here, what's—"

"James says you can't leave."

"Who told you that?" Katherine's eyes darted back to the girl but she kept the gun trained on the monstrosity in the corner. "Who told you to say these things?"

"James says you can't leave. You only think you can."

Katherine bit her lower lip, felt the weight and power of the shotgun in her hands. "You're trespassing," she said to the man, "and you've broken into this cabin, so we can add breaking and entering to the charges as well. Now answer me or I'll call the police and you can explain yourself to them."

The little girl smiled, amused.

Katherine took a step closer to the man. "I'll pull this trigger, you sonofabitch, don't think I won't." She shook the barrel of the shotgun in his direction to emphasize the danger it posed, but the man remained silent. "Do you have any idea what this would do to you at such a close range? Answer me, or so help me God we're going to find out. What is she talking about?"

"You have to stay," the little girl answered for him. "Here, with us."

"Answer me, goddamn it! What is she talking about?"

"You have to stay," she said again.

Katherine looked back at her. "What happened to your eyes?" she whispered. "What has he done to your eyes?"

Don't look at me, James called to her from the past. *Don't look at me.*

"No," Katherine said, answering herself. "No, this—this can't be."

"Stay with us." The little girl opened her arms. "Here, with *all* of us."

"Where is he?" she demanded. "He—James isn't here, he isn't here!"

"But you know he is. He's right in front of you. He's all around us."

Katherine turned and bolted into the cold, the world tilting and blurred as she ran through curtains of snow, her mind racing for solutions, explanations, anything that might make sense of this nightmare.

Nightmares can kill, James had once told her, running his hands over his scalp as if fascinated by the skull beneath it. *Madness, bad dreams— it's all the same. I never knew, I didn't believe it, but it's true, Katherine, it's true. I can make them one.*

As she ran with all her might, Katherine's vision distorted, and her heart beat with frightening power. Darting through the snow, she didn't take the time to consider in which direction she had headed. Staggering forward, her foot snagged on something just beneath the snow, and she tumbled into midair, landing several feet away and crashing into a large drift with tremendous force. Her body smashed through it and slid headlong into the blinding storm. She did her best to roll through the fall but the impact caused the shotgun to leave her hands. Most of the air in her lungs followed, exiting her body in a single rush.

Lost in the whiteout, the frenzied sensation of suffocating, of not being able to draw even a single breath, was the last thing she remembered before her head slapped the frozen ground.

The snow turned black and Katherine felt herself falling away into nothingness while James, his breath hot in her ear, whispered prayers she hadn't heard in years.

Pray the Lord your soul to keep, Katherine. Pray the Lord your soul to keep.

CHAPTER TEN

Carlo watched the woman, her lips again moving in silent prayer as the rosary beads slipped through her fingers. "Is Katherine in danger, Mrs. Covington?"

"You're *all* in danger, boy." Her tone assumed a more hostile edge, and her posture and expression followed suit. "Once these things are decided, only James can stop them. We're just pawns."

"Have you seen James since he disappeared?" Carlo pressed.

"You think he doesn't know I'm talking to you?"

Carlo glanced up at the windows on the second floor, but there seemed to be nothing lurking behind the dingy old curtains. "You have, haven't you?"

"You don't understand any of it. Do you even know where you are, boy? James isn't here with us." Spittle formed at the corners of Josephine's mouth. "We're *there*, with *him*."

Carlo started back down the stairs. This woman was clearly out of her mind, but even if only part of what she'd told him were true, he felt it warranted talking to Katherine about it as soon as possible. "You really should go back inside, Mrs. Covington," he said, hesitating at the car only long enough to look back once more at the house and the old woman on the porch swing. "If you don't, you're liable to freeze to death out here."

Josephine Covington stared in his direction with her milky eyes but said nothing.

The snow was coming down faster. Carlo slid behind the wheel, started the car and grabbed his phone. He dialed Katherine's home number but got a "circuits busy" recording, so he tried her cell phone. It went immediately to voice mail. "Hey, it's me," he said. "Give me a call back on my cell soon as you can. I need to talk to you."

He flipped the phone shut. As he pulled away from the house he saw Josephine still sitting on the porch swing, the wind rocking her slowly back and forth through the swirling snow.

While driving, Carlo replayed their conversation in his head. The problem was figuring out how much of what Josephine had told him was accurate and how much could be dismissed as the confused ramblings of a senile old woman. If there really had been a son—if Parker truly had existed at some point—and if he truly had drowned, or worse, *been* drowned by James, then surely the death of the Japanese boy at the lake hadn't been an accident either. But even if Parker had drowned, it didn't necessarily mean James had anything to do with it, and it certainly didn't prove he'd killed the Japanese boy or become some psychotic child killer either. Although tragic, couldn't the fact that both boys knew James before they drowned simply be coincidence?

And yet Josephine had seemed so certain.

I know James. I know his secrets.

Memories of James passed through his mind slowly, a slide show of glimpses and disjointed reminiscences. His face, his eyes, his smile, his lips moving, talking without making any sound like in a silent movie, his arms around Katherine; flashes of the three of them at the lake, in the sunshine, happy, oblivious.

"Who the hell were you?" Carlo mumbled.

We're just pawns.

It all slipped away, replaced by the sweep of windshield wipers battling the spitting, intensifying snow.

He was nearing the highway, his mind still racing, when the intrusive ring of the cell phone interrupted his thoughts. "Katherine?"

"It's Reg," a deep male voice answered.

Carlo was surprised to hear from him so soon after their meeting, particularly after the awkward way it had ended, but he recognized a tinge of guilt in Reggie's tone. "What's up?"

"Since that other info was dated and you seemed interested, I went ahead and did a quick background check on your boy's foster mother Josephine Covington. Figured I'd let you know and save you some time and trouble."

"Thanks, but I—"

"She died a year and a half ago."

A burst of nervous laughter escaped him. "What?"

"She's deceased. Josephine Covington."

"That can't be, I—that must be the wrong information or a mistake or something, because I was just—"

"There's no mistake, I've got it right here in front of me. She died a few months before James disappeared."

Flashes of the dream Carlo had the night before blinked in his mind. It was still blurry and indistinct, but he was certain he had glimpsed a memory of James watching him and laughing. He had a strange look about him, something between compassion and indifference, between pride and conviction.

"She was found dead at that address I gave you by a hospice worker," Reggie said. "Cause of death was listed as heart failure."

"But I was just there. I was just talking to her."

"Just talking to who?"

Carlo's hands had begun to shake so violently he slowed the car and turned off the road into the breakdown lane. "Josephine Covington. Not five minutes ago."

"Damone, I don't have time for this, okay?"

"She's old, and she's a wreck, but she's alive. Matter of fact, she told me—"

"I figured I'd let you know, that's all. I got to go."

"Hold up, this is important. She told me about a son they had, a boy named Parker who apparently—"

"I said I don't have time for this."

"Listen to me a minute, I—"

"No, man, you listen," Reggie snapped. "I don't know who the hell it was you think you were talking to, but it wasn't Josephine Covington. The woman is dead, you got it? She's been dead more than a year."

"She had a son, Reggie, a real son, and I think James might have—"

"You got a problem, Damone, you hear me? Get off the booze before it rots what little brain you got left. It's still daylight and you're on your ass. Think that's healthy?"

"I haven't had anything to drink but coffee."

"Get some help."

"You don't understand, I—"

"And for God's sake, get off the road before you kill yourself or somebody else, you damn fool."

"Goddamn it, Reg, just hear me out!"

The line turned to static and *Call Lost* scrolled across the face of his phone.

Carlo angrily tossed the cell onto the passenger seat and ran his hands through his hair. It was still damp from the snow. "This is insane," he muttered, heart pounding.

We're just pawns.

Like in a game, Carlo thought, a diseased and evil game.

"It has to be a mistake, that's all," he muttered to himself. "It... has to be."

Determined to prove just that, he dropped the car into *Drive*, pulled a U-turn, and sped back in the direction from which he'd come.

CHAPTER ELEVEN

During the spring and summer seasons, Katherine and James awakened early and almost always ahead of the guests. One particularly humid morning, they sat out on the steps having coffee while talking quietly and looking out over the lake, its surface smooth as a newly polished floor, placid and radiant beneath a slowly rising sun.

Though they had both been raised around the ocean, for James, the concept of swimming and communing with the water—whether it was the sea, the lake, a pool or even a walk in the rain—had never lost its allure. Katherine was a good swimmer, but never enjoyed the water to the extent James had. Over the years he had grown fond of the lake, clearly favored it, and rarely ventured to the beach. He seemed more connected to the lake in a physical and spiritual sense, while for Katherine, it was a pleasant but otherwise familiar experience, and therefore rather commonplace. Unlike James, Katherine still preferred the ocean, though she too rarely had time to go there.

"I love the ocean, but you never know what's swimming alongside you in the open water," he'd said on more than one occasion. "I think if most people realized what was lurking just beneath their toes out there, they'd never leave the beach."

"You should've never seen *Jaws*," she said jokingly.

"There's more out there than we've even begun to understand."

"Probably," she agreed. "Look at all the new species they keep finding in super-deep waters. But the worst anyone is liable to encounter while swimming at the beaches around here is a jellyfish or a sand shark, and even that's rare."

James had smiled at her the way he sometimes did, with a mixture of interest and just a hint of condescension, the latter of which irritated her to no end. "At least I know what's in the lake.

One can never be sure what's skulking around out in the ocean, Katherine, that's my point."

"Actually, I think we have a very good idea of what swims in these waters," she said, dropping in a condescending tone of her own. "The lake is beautiful, don't get me wrong, but the ocean is so majestic and sweeping. Besides, what kind of New Englander prefers lakes to the Atlantic Ocean?"

"The lake's safer."

The sun had just fully cleared the trees on the far side of the lake, and its rays shone down more powerfully, gliding across the smooth surface like perfectly skipped stones. "Some sections of the lake are awfully deep," she reminded him. "And it's not as if there's no life out there."

"That's not what I meant. It's not as easily..."

"Controlled?" she offered.

"The lake is just less mysterious, that's all I'm saying."

"But you love the mysterious."

This time, when he looked at her, his smile was gone, replaced instead with a strange look of concern. "Not always."

Katherine put her coffee down and slid closer to her husband. "We should go to the beach one of these nights. We used to go all the time when we were dating."

"That was before we owned this place." James slipped an arm over her shoulder and planted a kiss on her forehead. "Now we've got all we need right here."

"Remember that night we got caught out on the dunes in that horrible thunderstorm?"

He nodded. "You were terrified."

"So were you," she laughed, that night so many years before replaying in her mind. "I never saw such lightning. You held me so tight, and kept saying everything was going to be all right, even though I had the distinct feeling you were trying to convince yourself as much as you were me."

He took her chin in his hand and raised her head until her eyes met his. "You have no idea how much I wanted to make love to you that night."

"Then why didn't you?"

"There was something perfect and pure about huddling there

with our arms around each other," he said. "It was like we were two innocent children out there all alone."

"We were both over twenty at the time."

"Don't be so literal. You know what I mean. I didn't want to ruin it."

"It wouldn't have ruined it, James."

"But it would've changed it." He grabbed his coffee, took a long sip. "And I wanted to be able to remember it just the way I wanted it to be, the way I meant it to be. The way we are right now."

Katherine stroked the side of his face a moment then let her hand drop away. "I always liked your poem about that night."

"'Thunder and Tears,'" he said.

"Recite it for me?"

"Oh, please. It was just a silly love poem."

"It wasn't silly to me. Come on, recite it for me."

"You know I don't like to—"

"For me?"

James smiled and shook his head, as if he had no choice but to comply, and she suspected he probably hadn't. He hesitated a moment, looked off into the distance as if to retrieve the words from some far-off cue card, then began. "'*Do you recall endless dunes, desolate beaches and spears of lightning stabbing the sky, rolling thunder, crashing waves...the rain...and how we held each other tight? Or is it just a blurry chapter in a book never finished? It doesn't matter, I guess, the thunder and all. The memory of your touch is enough, somehow.*'"

"See? It's not the least bit silly," she said. "It's beautiful."

"You know I haven't written that sort of thing in eons."

"That was before your work became so dark and—"

"Serious, Katherine, it's called serious art...or at least my feeble attempt at it. Any jackass can write love poems or greeting card copy."

"You so rarely let me read your work these days, I wouldn't know anyway."

His demeanor noticeably changed. "It's not very good."

"I'm sure it's terrific. Why are you so down on yourself lately?"

James closed his eyes but said nothing, like the answer was too painful to voice.

"Sometimes you act as if you're trying to shield me from your work," she told him. "I almost get the impression you think you're protecting me from it or something."

"Maybe I am."

"Why would you feel the need to do that?"

When he again chose not to answer, Katherine put her coffee aside and reached for him. He purposely remained just beyond her touch.

Katherine returned her hands to her lap, and she and James sat quietly finishing their coffee, together yet apart, beneath the gentle caress of morning sun.

You were hiding from me even then, weren't you, James? Hiding all your demons, all your thoughts and fears and writings—your endless notes and scribbles in your journal—still hoping you could somehow escape all those things so vehemently pursuing you. But no one can outrun the night, can they, James? Not even with all your poems and prayers and alleged intellectual superiority. No one can outrun the truth. Not even you.

The past slept, slipped away to darkness.

Something wet tickled her face. The sky, gray and blurred through the falling flakes, came into focus above her as she opened her eyes, leaving the darkness of unconscious memories in favor of one more current. As her mind gradually cleared, Katherine remembered the cabin, the little girl and the man—she remembered running, falling, tumbling into the snow and everything going blank. She couldn't tell how long she'd been unconscious and lying in the snow, but she was soaked and cold and her head was spinning. With a great deal of effort, she struggled to her hands and knees. Shooting pains arced through her shoulders. Coughing and gagging for air, she forced herself to her feet. In a newly formed trough in the snow, she located the shotgun and retrieved it.

She looked around and only then realized she'd fallen from the edge of the parking area down a small dune and onto the shores of the lake.

It was so quiet here, so deathly quiet. The snow was heavier and falling faster than before, the air filled with big plump flakes.

Her breath regained, she made her way through the heavy snow and trudged back up the slight incline until she'd reached the parking area. In the distance, the cabins sat locked, snow-covered and undisturbed. All were dark.

She looked back at the lake.

Walking away from her, across the frozen surface of the lake, was a man. A child walked on either side of him, each holding a hand. A third child clung to the stranger's chest, legs clutching his waist and small arms wrapped around his neck to prevent himself from falling. The children on foot looked back at her in unison, but even at such a distance it was obvious only one possessed eyes that could see.

Katherine recognized the first as the little girl.

The second took a bit longer to identify through the snowfall, but even before his face came into full view, she knew it was the Japanese boy.

The third child slowly raised his head from the man's shoulder. She had never seen him before, yet the child looked at her as if he knew her well.

As the foursome continued moving away into the storm, the stranger finally looked back at her as well.

It was not the same man from the cabin.

"James," she whispered.

CHAPTER TWELVE

The porch swing sat empty, the house silent, still and already covered in snow.

This is ridiculous, Carlo thought. *There's a snowstorm going on, of course she wouldn't still be out here. Obviously, she's gone inside.*

He left the car and approached the house. None of the windows were filled with light, just dingy old curtains, all of them drawn, and the front door stood closed. A fresh layer of snow covered the porch, masking any tracks the old woman might have left as she hobbled back inside.

Carlo knocked on the door. It rattled in the casing with each blow, but even after numerous attempts and several minutes, no one answered.

She's old, he thought. *If she's upstairs, she probably can't even hear me knocking.*

He tried to peek through the nearest window, but the curtains were too thick and filthy to yield even a glimpse of what lay beyond.

Carlo returned to the front door and knocked again, this time with more force. Still, no one answered, so he tried the knob, and to his surprise, found the door unlocked. He gave it a slight push with his fingertips, and the door swung open a few inches. He leaned closer. "Mrs. Covington!" he shouted. "Ma'am, are you here?"

A gust of wind caught the door, swung it open farther.

Carlo stepped through into a small foyer. The interior of the house was as worn and neglected as the exterior. From his position just inside the door, he could see a large staircase a few feet in front of him. To his left was the remainder of the foyer, and an open doorway leading to some other part of the house, most likely the kitchen. To the right lay a spacious front room that had probably been used as a living room or den, but the floors were bare, and he saw no furniture or signs that anyone lived here. In fact, from all indications, no one had lived in this house for quite some time.

"Mrs. Covington?" he called again, his voice reverberating through the foyer and along the dusty staircase before trailing off into shadows at the top of the stairs.

Josephine Covington. She's deceased.

"Mrs. Covington!"

She died a year and a half ago.

Carlo approached the base of the stairs, put a foot on the first step and craned his neck in an attempt to see beyond the darkness on the second floor landing.

The shadows were too thick.

He stepped away from the staircase, and though he made a concerted effort to settle his nerves, couldn't shake a sudden feeling of dread.

In the empty house, the sounds of the mounting storm intensified, echoed through the vacant rooms and across the high ceilings. Each tick of icy snow hitting a windowpane, each gust of winter wind coursing through the field and assaulting the house, each creak of the aging foundation, was more conspicuous and profound than usual, more ominous than it should have been.

What sounded like slurred whispers bled from the walls, swirled around him then just as quickly fell silent.

Only the wind, Carlo assured himself. But his sense of dread grew stronger and fell over him like a heavy blanket draped across his shoulders, weighting him down.

Forcing himself forward, he moved toward the open doorway to the adjacent living room. The windows were tall and narrow, dressed in faded curtains. The floor was old hardwood—probably quite beautiful once—and against the far wall was a fireplace, a dusty and empty mantel above it.

Along the left-hand interior wall sat a casket.

Heart pounding, Carlo tried to comprehend what he was seeing. It was so small, it—how could such a thing be so small?

My God, he thought. *It's meant for a child.*

The diminutive casket was a high-gloss black color with ornate silver handles, the lid propped open to reveal a frilly satin interior. A kneeling stool had been placed in front of it, as if in anticipation of his arrival.

There was something inherently profane about a child's coffin, something unnatural and obscene. Something wicked. But there it was, spitting in the face of nature, a gruesome shrine to premature death, mocking all that was decent and just.

The dread crawled deeper, burrowed closer to the bone, and Carlo was suddenly confronted with the overwhelming feeling that someone was standing behind him. He could feel them breathing on the back of his neck.

He whipped around, hands raised defensively and balled into fists.

Nothing...no one...

Carlo turned back in the direction of the coffin, but without moving closer he couldn't tell if it was empty.

The wind whispered to him again, the words just beyond his comprehension.

His stomach twisted into a knot. He forced a swallow then very slowly crossed the large room until he was within a few feet of the casket. "God Almighty," he said bleakly, his breath snared in the base of his throat. "What the hell is this?"

A young boy lay within the small black coffin, dressed in a little gray suit. A set of rosary beads were draped across his folded hands and entwined in his fingers. The same beads Carlo had seen Josephine Covington praying with on the porch swing earlier. The boy, obviously embalmed, looked more like a doll than a human being, but had not decomposed at all. Even if this was Josephine's long-dead son Parker, it was impossible for the body to still be so well preserved after all these years.

Then what in God's name is happening here? Am I—could I be dreaming? Carlo wondered. *Could I be asleep?*

His body shivered violently, reminding him just how awake he was.

As Carlo stepped back, his feet slipped out from under him, but just before he went down he managed to regain his balance and stumble to the doorway. He looked back. The floor where he'd been standing was wet. At first he thought it might be snow he'd tracked in on his shoes, but there was too much of it.

A dripping sound turned his attention to the casket. Water leaked in a slow but steady stream from the underside of the coffin, hitting the floor to form a rivulet that ran across the room into a small puddle on the section of floor Carlo had occupied just seconds before.

Something creaked behind him. He staggered out of the room into the foyer just in time to see a shadow moving quickly across the top of the stairs. Subtle sounds of movement scurried overhead, like the pitter-patter of little feet.

Carlo reached to his belt for his cell phone, but it wasn't there. As he headed for the front door, he remembered angrily tossing the phone onto the passenger seat in his car after Reggie had hung up on him.

More garbled whispers circled him, this time emanating from the top of the staircase.

He nearly fell as he left the house in a frenzied rush, tripping across the porch and taking the front steps in one awkward giant step that planted him in the snow. His knees buckled on impact but he was moving so quickly he managed to stride right through it until he'd reached his car. As he fell against the side panel, he heard the front door slam shut.

Carlo turned back toward the house.

One of the upstairs windows facing him had changed. The curtains were open, and Josephine Covington, or something that looked like Josephine Covington, stood watching him with her milky eyes.

It's not real, what he'll show you.

The front door opened with a slow creak, drawing Carlo's attention from the window.

The little boy in the gray suit stood smiling at him innocently, his bloodless skin pale and powdered lips creased but held closed, sewn shut in death.

What James will show you—none of it's real.

Carlo felt himself coming apart, like someone had reached in through his chest and was slowly pulling the life out of him. The fear had grown to a point where he had become numb to it, his body relaxed now and embracing a desire to sleep, to escape. He could only wonder if this was what it felt like at the moment of death, when one finally succumbed to the reality of what was happening and no longer fought or ran, but instead quietly accepted destiny and whatever designs it had in mind.

Just like the lake itself, there is the surface, and there is what lies beneath.

Carlo slid to the ground, felt the cold snow against his legs as his eyes closed. But rather than darkness, he saw an image of himself climbing the stairs in the house, moving purposely up the old stairs and into a dark hallway. He saw himself follow it to a door, saw his hand reach out and open it to reveal an unkempt bedroom. He wanted to open his eyes, wanted to wake up, but the pictures in his mind refused to cooperate.

Josephine Covington's brittle and decaying body lay atop a filthy bed in that horrible old house, soiled and rotting as flies buzzed about noisily, the rosary beads with the gold crucifix again wrapped about her misshapen fingers. And those eyes—blurred by cataracts and seeing only the darkness of a past still haunting her, forever etched in her mind and filtered through the milky film coating what little vision remained—now wide and gazing forever into the black void separating this world from the next.

The visions finally released him, and Carlo's eyes fluttered open.

In the window, Josephine Covington began to rock back and forth, slowly at first, as if moving to the rhythmic beat of some slow distant song, then faster and faster still, until her body became a writhing blur convulsing about at inhuman speeds.

Something suddenly burst from her chest, something like bone— white and glistening—spraying the window with an explosion of blood and gore that concealed his view of her.

Carlo struggled to his feet, slipping through ice and snow as he frantically reached for the car door. Filtered through heavy snowfall, he could still see the little boy watching him from the front steps. But the innocent smile had become a demonic grin.

You don't understand any of it.

With a crazed look in his dead eyes, the boy vaulted from the steps and started toward him at a full run.

Carlo fell into the car and pulled the door closed behind him just as the boy leapt into the air, diminutive embalmed hands reaching for him.

And then it was over, absorbed into the snow and carried away on the wind.

Carlo found himself alone, no longer in the car but standing near the front steps of the house instead, his inert form covered in a growing layer of snow. No one in the windows, no little boy on the steps, no open front door, no coffins or ghostly whispers, only the squeak of the empty porch swing swaying in the wind.

James isn't here with us.

Trembling, Carlo slowly backed away.

We're there, with him.

There. The lake. Where Katherine was right now. By herself.

"No," he said softly. "Not by herself. You're there too. Aren't you, James?"

The house fell silent, harboring its secrets and concealing its ghosts. Only a relentless sense of foreboding remained.

Carlo ran for the car.

CHAPTER THIRTEEN

She reached the deck steps and climbed them on pure adrenaline, but Katherine was no longer running. The fear had evolved into something more, something so powerful and encompassing that her mind reacted with an odd serenity. Like a switch deep within her had been thrown, she functioned without really thinking about it, her body still racked with terror but moving to the commands of an internal automatic pilot.

Once she had slipped into the den, slammed shut the sliders and locked them, she briefly looked back out at the lake. The snow was coming down harder than ever, the flakes blowing about at the mercy of an increasingly harsh wind. The blizzard was no longer on its way. It was here.

The natural inclination was to get as far from this place as she could, but that was impossible now. The storm had seen to that.

Katherine didn't bother to check the phones. She knew they'd still be dead. Instead, she put the shotgun aside and sank down into a sitting position on the floor, her legs out in front of her and her back resting against the wall. "Get a grip," she said aloud, detesting the fear in her voice. "Come on, Katherine, get a goddamn grip, this is insane, it—it's *crazy.*"

Barney had curled up in a nearby recliner and only then come awake. He offered a dramatic yawn and a quizzical look, then after a lengthy stretch, hopped down, sauntered closer and sat next to her on the floor.

Still shivering, Katherine reached for him, pulled the cat onto her lap and felt his warmth wash over her. Her clothes were soaked through in some areas and merely damp in others, but the back of her head was cold and wet, the sodden hair dripping icy water along her neck in a slow but steady rhythm. Her hands and feet, in particular, felt frozen. She wrested free an old afghan from the back of the couch and vigorously dried her hair with a corner of it as best she could. With an annoyed grunt, Barney adjusted positions then settled against her chest and began to purr. Katherine wrapped them both in the remainder of the blanket, and gradually, her pulse slowed and the fear began to give way to rational thought. She considered that perhaps she'd only fallen in the snow, struck her head and had somehow been dreaming the entire scenario with the man, the little girl and all the rest. That had to be it. It *had* to be.

The alternative was too horrific to consider.

From her position she could see through the sliders to the flickering snow beyond, but little else. Still, the lake was there in the distance as always, silent and offering nothing. The same frozen lake she had seen James and those children walk across before the storm had consumed them.

"No," she whispered. "This is ridiculous. I have to stop this. This cannot be real, I—I have to stop this. Deep breaths and—and clear your mind—just clear your mind, yes that's it, clear your mind. Slow deep breaths. Slow. Slow deep breaths."

With the soft rumble of Barney's purr playing in her ear, Katherine closed her eyes and continued her breathing exercises, slowly drifting off to a calmer place, a safer place.

Or so she thought.

James was waiting, watching her from the dark dreamscapes of her mind. In these memories he appeared tired and drawn, like he had in the days just before he'd disappeared. He'd lost quite a bit of weight over the last few weeks, and but for the black saddlebags beneath each eye, he was deathly pale. This was a man who had not slept in quite a while—who had not been at peace in some time— and for whom the consequences had become cruelly apparent.

She remembered herself there as well, sitting at the kitchen table while he stared out the sliders with his bloodshot eyes, looking at the night as if it were looking back...and perhaps it had been. "You've been writing a lot lately," she said. When she spoke to her husband these days it was carefully, as his reaction was never something she could be certain of. "I've seen you writing in your journal. Are you working on new poems?"

James shook his head so slowly it was at first difficult to detect.

"What are you writing then?"

"The things in my head," he answered in a weak and raspy voice. "I have to get them out. It's the only way I know how to do it. Ever since I was a little boy, I've written things down. Thoughts, dreams, stories, poems, all of it written down, pounded out on old typewriters or scribbled here or there on pads and scraps of paper, like once I'd written it down I'd be free of it somehow."

"James, where do your poems come from?"

"I don't know. Where do your thoughts come from?"

"That's different."

"How so?"

"Because thoughts are different from things you write yourself."

"Are you sure?"

"Of course I'm sure. How can you write something and not—"

"Sometimes it's like they're being dictated to me from someone else, and I just write them down." He sighed heavily. "And yet, there isn't a detachment about it, the process, I mean, or the work itself. I'm connected to it very strongly, like the words come from somewhere deep within me, which I suppose they do. Still, beyond that, their origin remains a mystery to me in many ways."

"*Beyond* that?" she asked. "What is there beyond the depths of your own soul?"

"Heaven?" James shrugged. "Hell?"

Katherine felt a sudden chill. "Maybe writing about darkness and thinking about things from that perspective for so long is catching up to you, blurring things for you?"

"You mean things like reality and fantasy."

"Yes."

"Do you honestly believe those things aren't already blurred?"

"I think your work makes it worse for you."

"Ah," he said, a touch a humor seeping into his tone like a cloud passing over the moon, "the artist and his demons. Hardly original, my love, but often accurate, the concept of the artist confronted with his or her own artistic manifestations. Just as we garner good from what we do, we also garner bad. There's beauty in even the most simplistic art, but also a dark side to it. Just like the human experience, yes? Serious art always deals to some degree with the darker aspects of existence. How can it not? Can't have one without the other, can we? But then, we all pay a price one way or another for what we do, not just lowly artists. All of us."

Katherine nodded. "But the rest of us know where our demons come from."

"I imagine they all come from the same basic place within each of us, don't you?"

"I'm not so sure anymore. The words, the stories and poems you create, the themes and thoughts within them, how do they come to be?"

"I told you, I don't know where they come from. I only know they come."

"Stop for a while. If you focused on something else for a time, maybe you could—"

"Katherine," he said grimly, "you can't make people be who you want them to be without destroying who they really are in the process."

That may not be such a bad thing, she thought.

"Even now, don't you understand that?" James asked.

"I understand that I love you and that you love me." Emotion scratched at her throat. "I've built my whole world around you."

"I know, and so have I." James gently placed a fingertip against the glass slider, as if to touch the night just beyond it. "But worlds end."

The room came back into focus gradually, the snow spitting against the sliders, obscuring the lake. Barney, still snuggled against her chest, slowly raised his head and watched the snow with her. Under normal circumstances, he would have still been purring loudly in her arms, but he had grown silent, and apart from the howling winds blowing in off the lake, only the faint slow and steady cadence of his breath was audible. The cat no longer seemed spooked, but was not totally at ease either, like he was furtively anticipating whatever else the rising storm planned to spew forth, and cognizant that no precaution could deter the inevitable.

Lies, Katherine thought, *my entire life and marriage, lies. No children, few friends to speak of, guests that came and went and remained impersonal, only James and me and our cat and the lake. Our own little insolated world, apart from everyone and everything else, and I never questioned a moment of it until it was too late. Why did you want me all to yourself so often, James? Why did you have to be apart from so much of the world, from people in anything but a transient and superficial sense? Why did you always keep a subtle distance from children, even those at the lake, those visiting and playing all summer long? What evil did you carry with you, in your work, in your poetry, in your soul?*

Both a curse and gift, his voice answered.

Katherine shook her head, trying desperately to dislodge the memories of her husband holding the lifeless body of the Japanese boy.

Both, Katherine, do you understand?

A shadow crept across the steps, an unfamiliar and foreign movement amidst the snow-blurred sliders.

Inside me, spilling out of me. I couldn't stop even if I wanted to.

Katherine's heart crashed her chest and her bowels clenched, shooting pains firing through her intestines. She felt Barney's body stiffen suddenly, and he vaulted away from her, launching himself into the air and escaping the room with a scrambling run.

You see them.

Once in the doorway, Barney stopped, turned and crouched low, glowing eyes trained on the slider. He hissed and skulked backward into the next room.

You see them, don't you?

Katherine looked to the slider as she struggled to her feet.

Something moved again. Something slow, prowling near the door but just far enough into the snowy afternoon to remain obscured. She slowly reached for the shotgun, forced a swallow down her bone-dry throat, and felt the weight of the weapon in her cold hands. If only she could hold it still, if only she could stop this awful trembling.

Through the sea of flakes, a blur emerged then retreated, as if disoriented.

And Katherine...now they see you too.

"Stop this," she said aloud. "*Please,* James. Please stop this. Help me."

The wind surged, blowing snow harder against the glass and covering the slider with a film of slushy ice and foggy condensation.

"James?" She craned her neck in the hope of a clearer view.

Something brushed the glass, ran down along the pane in a slow scrape that squeaked like fingernails across her spine. Fingers. Old, gnarled, talon-like fingers, gliding slowly down the slider, leaving a trail in the slush, and a glimpse of what lay beyond it.

That face. *My God*, she thought. *I...I know that face. Where? Where have I seen it?*

And then it clicked. She'd only seen it once, and it had been years before, but there was no mistaking it.

"Josephine?"

Is she out there with you now, James? Is she there with you and the children, all of you bound and woven together in some perverse web of sightless dementia and darkness?

The old woman, forever frozen in agony, forever dead, pressed her face to the glass, mouth open in a silent scream, eyes coated in a slimy white shell, cataracts having consumed them entirely.

A rush of terror crashed through Katherine like a brutal gust of wind, and she buckled at the knees, the room whirling and tilting as she lost consciousness and tumbled to the floor.

The shotgun fell beside her and skidded away.

Just out of reach.

CHAPTER FOURTEEN

The farther back into Massachusetts Carlo went, the more treacherous the roads became. But he had to get to Katherine, and that left him no choice but to drive right into the heart of the blizzard. He stuck to the highway as often as possible, because on most state roads a fleet of enormous sanders and plows were out there with him, yellow strobe lights blinking through the whiteout in a losing battle to stay ahead of the snowfall.

He did his best to concentrate on driving and keeping the car on the road, and it helped to distract him from what he'd experienced at the old Covington house. But the fear remained, the confusion and disbelief mixed with a continual sense of dread and horror. He simply couldn't get his mind around what had happened in any consequential way, and yet, he knew damn well he hadn't been asleep, drunk or unconscious. He'd been wide awake. And nightmares weren't nightmares unless you were asleep. If they came to you while you were awake, they were something else entirely.

They were real.

But Carlo had never believed in such things—ghosts and demons, premonitions and hauntings and all the rest—he'd always dismissed them as nonsense, as the products of overactive imaginations. Now, he could no longer be quite so sure. He knew what he'd seen and experienced, but surely they had to be hallucinations of some kind. The salient questions were: Where had they come from, and who was responsible for their manifestation? Could James somehow be communicating with him, trying to influence him in some way? And if so, whether he was dead or alive, how was such a thing even possible? Such were the kinds of riddles the insane pondered endlessly in joyless state hospitals while awaiting their next round of meds.

He suddenly knew all too well what Katherine had meant

about contagious insanity. Perhaps the insanity that had claimed James and that Katherine feared was becoming her reality as well, had turned its attention to him. He'd been so smug when they'd discussed it, so sure she was exaggerating or reading too much into things, and now the same madness was nipping at his heels.

Carlo's hands clutched the steering wheel so tightly they'd begun to ache, and his pulse throbbed in his temples, leaving him a bit lightheaded and fatigued. Despite the cold, his brow was coated in a thin film of perspiration, and though the shaking that had throttled him from head to toe earlier had lessened, the muscles in his neck, shoulders and arms remained tense and sore.

He knew there was a bottle of whiskey in the glove compartment. Only a pint, but it was full. Just in case, he'd told himself when he'd put it there. *Just in case I need it.*

"That's the last thing you need," he said, blinking away a bead of perspiration and focusing on the endless white beyond the windshield. Understandably, after what had happened, he knew a drink would help relax him, but that wasn't the point. He didn't want a drink. He needed one. *My God*, he thought. *I actually do. I need it.*

The shakes returned, only this time fear alone was not the culprit.

"What the hell have I done to myself?" He pawed the sweat from his eyebrows quickly, so his hand wouldn't be off the wheel too long. When had things gotten so out of control with his drinking? Hiding bottles in his car? When had it become *that* bad? "Focus, just—just focus and it'll be all right," he insisted, bartering with himself. "You don't need it like that. It's not like that, you—you're not that bad, man, hang in. Later, I—soon as I get to Katherine's—I'll have a good long sip or two. Just get there first, you useless bastard, for once in your fucking life do the right thing."

The rear tires slipped a bit and the car fishtailed. He gently tapped the break and the car corrected its aim. He continued on, straining through the thick flakes for any sign of his exit. In these conditions he was still just under an hour from Katherine, and that was assuming he could even get that far. If the highways were this bad, there was no telling how impenetrable the back roads might be.

Ignoring the flashing images still haunting his memory, he snatched his cell phone from the passenger seat and dialed Katherine's home number. As before, he got a "circuits busy" message, so he tried her cell. Like his last attempt, it again went directly to voice mail. This time he disconnected without leaving a message. He had to reach her somehow. Josephine Covington's voice replayed in his mind, telling him they were all in danger. And the thought of Katherine alone and trapped at the lake made his skin crawl. He had to get her out of there, had to find a way to—*Marcy*! She was only about ten minutes from the lake. He didn't know her home number offhand, but remembered programming it into his phone so he wouldn't forget it when they'd made their disastrous attempts at dating. He located it in his directory and hit *Dial*.

She answered with her typical degree of epic perkiness. "Ice Station Zebra!"

He'd never been happier to hear Marcy's grating voice. "Marcy, it's me, Carlo."

"Hey, how's it going, sugar?"

"Have you heard from Katherine?"

"I tried to call her awhile ago just to chat but I think the lines out that way might be down. Figures with all this snow, my God have you ever seen anything like this? I mean, it just keeps coming. I don't think it's ever going to—"

"Marcy, listen." His signal was beginning to crackle. "I need you to do something for me if you can, all right? I'm in Rhode Island and—"

"What are you doing in Rhode Island? Nice day for a drive, dipshit!"

"Look, I have some information for Katherine, information she needs to know. I'm on my way to her place now, but I'm still a ways off and I'm worried about her. I can't go into it right now but—"

"You're breaking up on me," she said. "It's no wonder in this storm. I don't know what it's like in Rhode Island but—wow—you should see it here! And it's only getting worse. I mean, it wasn't all that bad when I first got up but now it's crazy, it's like something out of a movie or something. That's why I said Ice Station Zebra when I answered the phone!" She laughed heartily, clearly amused with herself. "Remember that movie? Rock Hudson was in it. I always liked him. Anyway, if Katherine's lines are down she shouldn't be out there all cut off from everybody. I couldn't even get her on her cell. Did I tell you I tried her on her cell too? No luck."

Certain she would have to stop to take a breath at some point he waited for his opening then pounced. "Marcy, can you go over there and check on her? Do you think you can still get through?"

She answered him, but the signal faded, and he wasn't able to make out her response.

"Say again, Marcy, I'm losing you!"

"I said, yeah, I can go pick her up if you want! I just bought a tank! You won't believe this thing, it's huge! Trust me, I can get anywhere! Even in this crap!"

"I'm on my way there now," Carlo yelled into the phone. "I'll meet you there, okay?"

"Cool, we can all come back to my place and get shitfaced! I mean, it's a frickin' blizzard, what the hell else is there to do, right? We'll raid my bar and—oh!—I have some kick-ass frozen pizzas we can—"

"Just get your ass over there and make sure she's all right!"

Dead air answered him, and for a second he thought they'd been disconnected.

"Hey, Carlo?" she finally asked, her tone a bit more concerned. "You sound really stressed, is everything okay?"

"Go now and I'll explain everything when I get there, okay?" Again, dead air answered. "Okay? Marcy?"

The call was lost.

"Hang on, Kate." Carlo snapped the phone shut. "I'm coming."

CHAPTER FIFTEEN

Words came to her through the darkness. Katherine had seen them before, written as a poem called "Down" in a book of poetry James had authored. But now the words were whispered in her ear in a voice that could only belong to her husband.

"I can see your thoughts... Hear your tears... Taste your sighs... Feel your terror... So rancid and cold... Decaying slowly... Just beneath me... Gentle whispers... Dancing numbly through my mind... Eyes rolling... Flooded with disbelief... Legs cramping... Ankles locked behind my back... Posed like store-window lovers... Left on display... Soiled, red and scarred... An everlasting union... A testament to my blood... Seeping quietly... Down."

As his voice dissipated, so did much of the darkness.

Katherine's body was slick with perspiration. She had apparently kicked the single sheet off earlier at some point and now lay exposed. James was nude too, sitting on the bed next to her, smiling and gently stroking her hair. He leaned closer, kissed her, his lips soft and warm, slightly wet. His hands caressed her thighs, his breath brushed her neck, and then he was blending into focus above her, his expression at once sad and intense.

As he entered her, his hands moved across her face and came to rest over her eyes.

Darkness closed in around her again as he pushed himself deeper still, and in her mind she saw the little blonde-haired girl, blind eyes blinking slowly. Eyes James had given life to. Even in the shadows of his mind, with all it had created and concealed, he hadn't wanted anyone, any*thing* to see him.

Tell me, Katherine, what do you suppose demons dream?

Just beyond the little girl, stood a young boy she did not recognize. But as he drew closer and the little girl vanished into the deeper darkness, Katherine knew he was the same boy she'd seen James carrying across the frozen lake. He was a very troubled-looking child, dressed in a gray suit.

"Who are you?" she whispered.

The boy stood watching silently for a time, and then he too faded into the darkness.

"I'm you," James answered for him. "And you are me."

He fucked her harder, his thrusts angry and violent. She raised her legs a bit higher and tried to clamp her knees against his sides in the hopes of slowing him, but he was too deep inside her. "You're hurting me," she gasped. "James, you—you're hurting me."

Bracing himself on either side of her head with his hands, he pushed himself up until his arms had locked. Arching his back, he slammed into her again and again, dropping his head and watching her breasts heave and bounce with each thrust.

When it was finally over, what followed were a few moments of confusion, as Katherine's mind did whatever it could to process what was happening to her into something logical and coherent. The possibilities streamed through her in rapid-fire fashion, one atop the next.

This is not happening. There is no one in the room but you and Barney. James is dead. Don't be afraid because this cannot be. Ignore it. Think of something else, distract yourself and it will all go away.

But Katherine knew better.

The final night played out before her mind's eye like a film, the last night she had seen her husband as fresh in her memory as it had been more than a year ago.

She had found James nude and sitting before the fireplace, pulling items from a large cardboard storage box and tossing them into the flames. He sat passively as they were consumed, saying nothing. Most were various notebooks filled with unfinished poems and stories, others actual journals and small press, independent or academic-based publications that had featured his work now and then over the years. The rest were his published collections.

"What the hell are you doing?"

He didn't bother to turn and look at her, or attempt to conceal what he was doing. Instead, he continued to pull items from the box and casually fling them into the fire.

"James, stop it," she demanded, moving closer.

"Leave me alone, Katherine."

She stood watching him a moment, unsure of what to do. It

seemed the only book safe from the flames was his journal, which he had next to him on the floor but apart from the other items, making it clear that for some reason, he planned to spare it. "Why are you doing this? That's your life's work you're throwing away."

"None of it matters," he said in monotone. "It never did. I know that now."

"That's not true."

"You have no idea what's true and what isn't."

She crouched down but remained a few feet away from him. "I want you to stop. Will you stop this for me? Please?"

"Why would you care? You can't even begin to understand any of this."

"We're going to get you some help, James. This has gone on long enough. I'm going to take you to a doctor and—"

He motioned with one hand, a lazy flicking motion clearly intended to dismiss her. "I love you, Katherine, but *Christ* you're so fucking stupid sometimes."

She rose to her feet and tightened the belt on her robe, though it didn't need tightening. "Who the hell do you think you're talking to? I'm your wife, how dare you speak to me like that?"

"Yes. How dare I?"

"I will not continue to live like this, James. You need help. Serious help. You're mentally ill. Stupid as I may be, I love you, and I'm willing to help you however I can. I suggest you accept it."

"And if that simply isn't possible? What then, Katherine the Great?"

Her eyes turned to steel. "Then fuck you."

James nodded, eyes transfixed on the flames. "I'm not who you thought I was, and I'm not *what* you thought I was." He tossed another booklet into the fire. "I'm not even who I thought I was. You should pack your bags and you should get away from here, Katherine, while I'm still willing to let you. Our life together is over. It's done. I'd give anything to change it, but nothing can put it back together again because nothing can put *me* back together again. Nothing can ever make it real again."

Her vision of him distorted through her tears. He was right. The man she had known and loved was gone, lost and replaced with this new version. The James she knew was kind and gentle and loving. Not…this. "You need help, James. There are people that can help you if you'll let them."

"I can do things."

Katherine moved closer. "What do you mean? *Do things?*"

"Things human beings cannot do. Things you could never understand even if I was able to explain them to you. What does that tell you?"

It tells me you're insane.

"It'll be all right," she said. "If only you'll—"

"You have no idea how I wish it didn't have to be this way, my love. But nothing will ever be all right again." He dug into the box, pulled free a digest-sized magazine and pitched it into the fireplace. "Wanting it, wishing it, willing it to be so isn't enough. Not anymore. It's come apart, Katherine. I can't do this anymore. I—I understand that now. I can't deny it. I can't run from it anymore."

"What are you talking about?"

"You can't understand, and I'm grateful for that, as you should be."

"Why would I be grateful for losing you? You're my husband. I'm your wife."

He bowed his head. "Not anymore."

"I love you."

"I love you too, and I always will. But I…I have to end it now, there's no other way. It can't last forever, not like you want it to, but we will be together forever, Katherine, in another way."

"You would never hurt me intentionally like this," she insisted.

He turned from the fire, and from the look in his eyes, she could no longer be sure.

"It's my nature," he said softly.

Katherine hugged herself against the sudden cold. "What do you want me to do? I—I feel so goddamn helpless, James, what—what do you want me to do?"

"Run," he whispered. "Run, Katherine. *Run.*"

She recalled fleeing to their bedroom, locking the door and sitting on the bed. Emotion overwhelmed her and she wept quietly for what seemed a very long time. She heard James muttering beyond the closed bedroom door, but was unable to make out the specifics of what he was saying. Even when an occasional word or two was audible, they sounded like some foreign language she'd never heard before, and he spoke them in an odd cadence that sounded almost like chanting...or prayer.

Later, while lying in bed still clothed and unable to sleep despite the hour, she heard him walking around the house, his footsteps slow and uncharacteristically heavy, plodding, as if he was slowly pacing back and forth. Waiting for something, perhaps, or simply waiting out the darkness for one more night. Toward the end James had only slept during the day, as he had become too frightened of the dark to sleep.

Eventually, the sounds receded and silence returned to their home.

In the morning, James was gone.

Katherine opened her eyes and the memories spiraled off, left her gradually, the way smoke from recently extinguished candles twists into the air.

She heard the sound of slowly dripping water but couldn't seem to locate exactly where it was coming from.

At some point Barney had returned. He was asleep and curled up beside her on the floor where she'd fainted. She rolled over a bit, felt her head swim. Her fingers stroked the cat's fur. At that moment she needed something concrete and real to hold on to. Carefully, she nudged Barney. He sighed, lifted his head and looked up at her sleepily. Odd, she thought. The cat had sensed things before, but now...

Her eyes slowly swept the dim room.

Nothing had happened. Yet.

But even before she detected the odd smell, or realized that the steady dripping sound was coming from *inside* the house and not out, she knew she and Barney were not alone.

CHAPTER SIXTEEN

Carlo had crossed the Blissful Point town line more than half an hour before, but because the roads were so bad he was still a distance from the lake. He was grateful his old car had made it this far in such taxing conditions, though, as its general reliability was questionable on the best of days. Far as he could tell, he was getting closer to the road that lead out to Katherine's, but he was only able to make out occasional landmarks. The windshield wipers could no longer keep up with the barrage of flakes, visibility was down to less than a few feet, and a violent and incessant wind assaulted the car, rocking it back and forth and making control at anything other than a slow crawl all but impossible.

He hadn't seen another car or truck since he'd left the highway. Man and animal both had taken shelter. Everyone, it seemed, but him.

Though the things he had experienced in Rhode Island continued to haunt his mind, offset now and then by whispers reminding him of the whiskey bottle in the glove compartment, it took every ounce of concentration Carlo could muster to maneuver through the storm and rising accumulation. Even at slow speeds, the deeper he ventured into the wooded area leading out to the lake, the harder it became to continue.

There had been plenty of huge snowstorms in the area over the years, and Carlo had witnessed many of them. But he'd never seen anything like this. For the first time since he'd set out, his head had cleared enough to consider how dangerous an undertaking this was. People died in weather like this, in areas like this. They froze to death in their cars.

The idea of a drink was more appealing by the minute. *Just one quick pull to settle your nerves*, the voice in his head suggested. *Just one and you'll be able to think.*

He fought the urge to even glance at the glove compartment and kept his focus on the windshield. The car groaned, rocked then surged forward, as if it had momentarily slipped out of gear. He gently tapped the brake then returned his foot to the gas. With great difficulty, the car continued on, but Carlo knew it wouldn't take him much farther.

Through the snow, he glimpsed a familiar old roadside sign that directed tourists to the resort. A small portion of it was still visible above the snow drifts, so he turned and did his best to follow a path where he assumed the dirt road beneath was hidden. He knew from his location he was less than a mile from the lake, but he seriously doubted he'd be able to drive the rest of the way. Visibility was close to nonexistent, and the snow was becoming deeper and thicker.

Within seconds the car ground to a halt, but Carlo kept the engine running and the wipers going as a strange hulking presence on the road ahead emerged through the whiteout. He leaned closer to the windshield for a better look, squinting through the storm at the dark mass. It was difficult to gauge distances, but he guessed it was perhaps fifteen yards ahead of him. Had the snow not stopped his progress, there was a good chance he might've run right into it. Its black coloring and sheer size were the only reasons he'd seen it.

After watching it for a few moments, he realized it had to be a vehicle of some kind, probably a large truck or an SUV. But surely something that size could've continued on, so why was it stopped in the middle of the road?

Oh, Christ, he thought. *Marcy.*

Carlo opened the door but it caught against a drift. He gave it a hard shove with his shoulder and it swung open far enough for him to climb out. As he did, a freezing gust of wind slammed his face with spikes of icy snow that felt like tiny needles. Even before he'd cleared the car, his face and hands began to sting and his eyes were watering. The wind was so constant and loud he could barely hear himself think, and were it not for the snow up to his knees, it would've knocked him over.

He trudged forward toward the SUV, sinking at times in snow drifts nearly to his waist. The deeper he sank the tighter the snow closed in around him, and the colder he became. If he lost his balance and fell into snow this deep and thick, the odds that he'd be able to get back to his feet were slim. He'd die out on this road and probably not be found for days.

Plodding at a slow but steady pace, he did his best to keep the SUV in his line of sight. In a storm of this magnitude becoming completely disoriented was not only possible, it was likely.

Eventually, he reached the SUV. The engine was off but there appeared to be no damage to the vehicle. The accumulation across the hood and roof suggested it had been parked out there awhile, but unlike his car, where the snow had been halfway up the doors, the SUV sat much higher and should've been able to continue on. It made no sense, why would Marcy simply stop in the middle of the road?

Carlo pounded on the driver-side door, knocking away large chunks of frozen snow. Once he'd located the handle, he pulled it, and the door opened.

The cab was empty but for a leather purse lying on the seat.

He climbed up into the front seat then closed the door behind him, shutting out the wind, snow and cold. A violent shiver throttled him from head to toe, but passed quickly. He rubbed his hands together furiously until he'd caught his breath and could again feel his fingers. Carefully, he next cleared his face of ice and snow.

The keys were still in the ignition. He turned them and the engine kicked on.

Techno dance music blasted from the stereo, nearly sending Carlo through the roof. He quickly shut the stereo off and turned the heater on instead. Wave after wave of warm air washed over him, and though his jeans were still wet and caked with frozen snow, it helped weaken the chill and settle his nerves.

He had no doubt this was the new SUV Marcy had told him about, but to be sure, Carlo grabbed the purse on the seat and rifled through it. The wallet inside held Marcy's driver's license and several credit cards with her name on them.

But then where the hell had she gone? She wouldn't just stop and abandon the SUV for no reason.

Something had forced her to stop.

Carlo gave a quick look around but could find no sign of struggle inside the vehicle and no damage to the exterior.

He opened the door and stood up in the doorway, bracing

himself against the top of the door. Any tracks Marcy had left upon exiting the vehicle had long been covered over. Carlo screamed her name twice, but could barely hear himself over the wind.

He dropped back behind the wheel, shut the door and switched on the wipers. As they cleared the windshield he again pawed the snow and ice from his eyes and face. He dropped the SUV into *Drive* and started forward, surprised at how easily it cut through the deep snow.

He continued on, doing his best to keep an eye out for Marcy. If for some unknown reason she'd walked the rest of the way to the lake, he could only assume she was either already there, or that he'd come across her on his way. Though he sat higher in the SUV than he had in his car, visibility wasn't much better. But Carlo saw no signs of anyone of anything, so he increased speed and blew through the drifts, confident now that he'd reach the lake within a minute or two.

Until he saw something in the road.

A child in a winter coat standing perfectly still, a hood pulled up over its head to conceal its face.

The child had materialized from the sea of snow so quickly that Carlo could only react instinctively, slamming the brakes and jerking the wheel, which sent the SUV careening off into the enormous snowdrifts on the side of the road.

An explosion of powdery snow erupted all around him as he hurtled directly for the forest, the trees growing larger and racing toward him in the windshield like some carnival ride gone amok. Carlo stomped the brakes again and yanked the wheel back in the opposite direction, but it was too late.

The horrible sounds of impact detonated in his ears, and a stampeding darkness closed in around him, swallowing the light in a furious rush.

CHAPTER SEVENTEEN

The slow drip of water was coming from inside the house, as was the strange smell wafting about. Both were real.

Katherine's eyes shifted, found the sliders. Snow still pelted them, and in the glimpses of distant and steadily darkening sky beyond, despite the plethora of flakes churning through it, a sliver of barely perceivable moonlight struggled for attention.

It would be dark soon. Where had the day gone?

The dripping sound continued...steadily...slowly. And the peculiar smell grew more pungent. It was an earthy odor Katherine had noticed now and then on the shores of the lake, mostly in the dead of summer. Normally unremarkable, it seemed commonplace out-of-doors but invasive and more overt once inside.

"James?" she whispered.

Barney stood up, stretched then sauntered to a nearby chair and took up position there. He curled up and returned to sleep, either unaware or unconcerned with what apparently haunted only Katherine now.

You can't leave, Katherine.

The shotgun still lay on the floor, just beyond her reach.

You never really could.

She slumped to the side and extended her arm until she could touch the shotgun. With a subtle push of her foot, her bottom slid across the floor, drawing her closer. Her hand closed over the gun.

Because there's nowhere to go.

Slowly, she dragged the shotgun back across the floor and returned to her upright sitting position. Bringing the weapon with her and onto her lap, she clutched it with both hands and let the barrel rest down near her knees.

There never has been.

Her body trembled and her mouth went dry.

And there never will be.

If the dripping sound and the smell were real, why then did his voice still echo in her head, disguised as her own thoughts?

See the truth, Katherine…see the truth.

In the hushed silence and partial light, with the shotgun held tight, she obeyed.

A vision surfaced through the darkness…

No longer in the house, she was lying outside on the back lawn, enjoying what seemed to be a clear and sunny summer morning. There were no guests about, and all was quiet. Even the normal symphony of birdsongs in the nearby forest was absent, casting the area in an eerie, unnatural silence. Katherine ran a hand through the lush grass as the sun washed over her, its rays revealing natural auburn highlights in her otherwise chestnut-colored hair. But for a pair of old cutoff denim shorts, she was nude, and a summer tan that covered the rest of her body left her breasts looking far more pallid than they actually were.

Before she could fully comprehend what was happening, the sound of someone approaching caught her attention. Katherine cupped and covered her breasts with her palms then looked up, but she was not wearing sunglasses and could only squint into the bright rays.

A hand reached for her, partially blocking the glare.

James, slightly blurred by the sunshine over his left shoulder, smiled down at her. He too wore only a pair of shorts. He looked vibrant, happy and healthy, like he had so very long ago. At least on the surface, this was the James she had once known and loved.

"You're so beautiful," he said tranquilly. "From the moment I saw you, I thought you were the most beautiful woman I'd ever seen. And as the years went by you became even more beautiful with age. Your face, your body, sometimes they overwhelmed me to the point where I could hardly stand it. I felt like I'd die if I didn't—"

"James, I—"

"Take my hand."

Katherine did so, and he gently pulled her to her feet. She used her free arm to cover herself. "I'm afraid."

"I understand," he said.

Still holding her hand, James escorted her across the backyard.

Katherine followed, allowed him to lead her, but as they neared the side lawn, where their laundry hung on lines, she hesitated. On this day, several bed sheets fluttered gently in the soft breeze blowing in off the lake. Like the world around them, James was faintly hazy, as if seen through a camera lens smeared with petroleum jelly.

Sound remained different here as well, filtered and softened.

"You don't have to cover yourself," he told her.

Self-consciously, Katherine let her arm fall. They continued walking.

"I lived without fear for so long I almost forgot what it was like," James explained. "But it's a full circle, like life itself, really. With youth comes innocence, and with innocence comes fear. In some ways, it's a natural component of childhood. But then we age. We become jaded and arrogant and we forget about fear. We become young adults and we feel a false sense of immortality. Fear subsides, becomes something we experience only in the most outrageous situations. Those things that terrified us as children are conquered, it seems, and we knock them aside like petty foolishness no longer worthy of our concern. Remember how you felt in your late teens and well into your twenties, Katherine? Untouchable and wonderfully alive in a way we never feel again…until we cross into our thirties and forties and something happens. A change occurs, and arrogance is replaced with susceptibility. One's mortality is no longer conceptual, it's a certainty. Vulnerability rears its ugly head, and it grows stronger and stronger the older we become. Without warning, the fear is back and stronger than ever. And it's more calculating and clever, more devious. What's worse, you come to realize it was never really gone in the first place. It's only been sleeping."

James and Katherine stopped just short of the hanging linens. Bright sunshine broke over the distant tree line beyond the house, casting the world in an exquisite golden hue. The sheets on the lines danced in the breeze, moving with the fluidity of water and rippling like waves. Though Katherine had seen these old sheets dance playfully in the breeze countless times before, there was something different about them this time. She found herself mesmerized by their willowy motion, and soon understood there was something more there than she first realized.

This time, as the sheets flapped lazily about, they allowed an occasional glimpse of what lay behind and between them.

Children.

The sheets fluttered and swayed to reveal their presence then just as quickly concealed them, repeating the process again and again as the breeze continued to slip up from the lake and scurry toward the forest. The little Japanese boy, the blind girl, and others she had not seen before, their dead eyes burrowing right through her, stood staring back at Katherine in silent vigil, there then gone again, swallowed by the swirling sheets.

Fear rose in Katherine, and James must have sensed this, as he tightened his grip on her hand reassuringly. "I'm with you," he said, as if this should have comforted her somehow.

Katherine watched the sheets. Their ballet continued, but the children were gone.

"Come with me to the lake," James said.

She pulled her hand free of his. "No."

"There's no other way."

"Who are the children, James? Who are they? Who is the man in the dark overcoat? What—what do they want?"

"Come with me to the lake," he said again.

"If I go with you I'll die." She looked out at the water. "I'll die in the lake."

James reached out and gently cupped the side of her face. "You won't die, my love."

"I will," she insisted, tears welling in her eyes. "I will, I—I *will*."

"No." He took her hand and started toward the shores of the lake.

"James, don't." Katherine staggered about behind him, pulled along like a disobedient child. "Please, James, don't."

Together they stumbled into the cool water. The farther James took her, and the deeper the water became, the less Katherine fought him. There seemed little use.

When the water had reached their waists, James stopped and took her in his arms, holding her bare chest against his own. He felt odd to her, his body cold and rigid, and beneath the surface of the water, she felt him harden against the front of her thigh. As he took her deeper she attempted to pull away, but his grip on her tightened.

His face brushed hers as they drifted into water well over their heads, and Katherine clung to him in an effort to stay afloat. He held her as well, and kicked in long slow strokes that sent them gliding farther and farther toward the center of the lake.

"Please," she said, the water breaking over her mouth. "I don't want to die."

"It's all right, Katherine," James whispered. "We're eternal."

CHAPTER EIGHTEEN

At first, sound returned to him in distorted waves, like a crackling radio signal struggling through heavy static and interference. Though Carlo had no awareness of time and place, he realized his auditory senses were again functioning. Before, there had been only silence behind the black veil that had fallen over him. Now that silence had been altered, albeit subtly, and had transformed unintelligible static from slurred babble to discernable language. He was hearing a distant voice—little more than a soft echo from the bottom of a well—but definitely a human voice, he was sure of it. Carlo strained to listen.

"We're sorry." The voice was female, and quite composed. "Your call cannot be completed as dialed. Due to a severe snowstorm, service to several areas has been temporarily interrupted. We apologize for any inconvenience and have technicians working to resolve the problem as quickly as possible. If you need further assistance, please stay on the line or press pound for more options."

No sight, no other sound, just that same detached female voice.

Through the darkness came the unexpected sensation of taste, but Carlo still had no sense of physical self, so it seemed completely independent of him. For all he knew he was floating in space, unconscious and trapped in some bizarre sleep state. Maybe even dead, he thought. The taste grew stronger, bringing with it an awareness of his mouth, teeth, tongue and throat. He willed his tongue to move, and it did, tasting more. Metallic and familiar, the substance coated his tongue and trickled along the back of his throat like syrup.

Blood, he heard himself say.

No, he—he had only thought the word.

Light flashed before him in quick intervals to create a strobe effect, but within seconds the intervals had grown longer and begun to linger, each burst of light allowing his vision to clear a bit more each time. He blinked repeatedly in the hopes of hurrying the process along, but everything remained slightly out of focus.

The serene voice echoed in his head again. "We're sorry. Your call cannot be completed as dialed. Due to a severe snowstorm, service to several areas has been temporarily interrupted. We apologize for any inconvenience and have technicians working to resolve the problem as quickly as possible. If you need further assistance, please stay on the line or press pound for more options."

And then nothing remained but the slow cadence of his breath and an otherwise uncanny silence.

Darkness returned. Had he closed his eyes?

After a few moments his mind began to fill with more thoughts and memories. Disjointed and independent of one another, they trickled through his head like raindrops before eventually merging to form complete phrases and sentences. Carlo remembered his cell phone. Had he attempted to make a call while semi-conscious? He wondered where the phone might be—it had to be nearby—but he had no context in which to frame these thoughts because he still had no clear idea of where he was.

From within the dark void came a clicking sound and another voice. "Operator Assistance."

"Operator?" His voice this time, but raspy, like he needed to clear his throat.

"Operator Assistance," the voice said more forcefully. "Is anyone on the line?"

"Operator," Carlo managed, "I've…"

I've what?

Another clicking sound was followed by a dial tone.

Carlo forced his eyes open. Light flickered into the void a second time, tiny pinholes of it that gradually expanded to allow more and more illumination in the darkness. Colors and shapes came to him as well, but as before, everything was blurred. He did his best to follow the sound of the dial tone, and eventually located his cell phone a few feet away from him, lying there open.

Though his vision had improved, something else was wrong. He couldn't quite put his finger on it, but something was definitely off. He shifted his eyes forward, and with his head still swirling, realized he was looking through some sort of large frame with a smooth surface and a strange configuration just beyond it.

Across his entire plain of vision was static, like snow on a television.

The sensation of pain suddenly joined that of taste, and a stabbing spasm fired through his head, across his temple and down into his jaw. Instinctively, he attempted to bring a hand to his head, and though he was able to do so, the angle was all wrong.

His hand had come from above his head rather than below it.

How could...

I'm hanging.

He wiped his eyes with the same hand, felt a sticky wetness gather between his fingers. His vision cleared a bit more. Crimson stained his hand and the blood taste became stronger. Carlo blinked and squinted until the blurriness sharpened significantly.

I'm...upside down.

Carlo realized he was looking through the blown-out windshield of an SUV at a section of snow-covered pavement. The configuration just past it was a row of trees signaling the start of the forest on that side of the road.

It wasn't static he was seeing, it was literal snow, still falling, snowflakes blowing about all around him. He could feel them now, along with the blood, wet against his face.

His mind slowly came around. More thoughts formed, and the difference between the here and now and memory was gradually becoming more distinct. His head was clearing, his memories returning, bringing him back to where he was and how he had gotten there.

Carlo tried to move again but this time his body refused to cooperate. The darkness returned, swallowing him and pulling him under. He did not fight the darkness. He chose instead to swim into it, embracing it so he might emerge on the other side where light and coherent thought would set him free of this black hole.

He was cold, so very cold. And all was quiet.

Trapped behind thick black walls, Carlo embraced the temporary sanctuary as memories materialized before him like ribbons unfurled.

James. In the end, this man with whom his best friend had spent years, slept with and held in her arms countless times, with whom she had shared so much, was someone she'd hardly known at all. As Katherine suggested to him on her last visit to his apartment, how well did anyone ever truly know anyone else?

How well do any of us even know ourselves? he wondered.

The darkness seemed fluid now, moving gracefully, slowly. Though Carlo could see nothing but endless waves of black, he knew he was being watched from somewhere nearby. He could feel it.

More memories unraveled before him, old blankets shaken open, the dirt and dust and debris trapped within, exposed.

There had been a child in the road.

He remembered swerving to avoid hitting the child, remembered hanging upside down and being trapped in an SUV—Marcy's SUV—with blood running down his throat and across his face. And for the first time since the crash, Carlo remembered fear.

Floating away from the darkness, he pushed through the black veils and back into the light.

White. So much white.

From one extreme to the other, he thought.

The SUV had hit a tree, apparently flipped over and skidded back out into the road, where it came to rest in the heavy snow. And now Carlo hung inside it, his head resting against the roof.

Move, he told himself. *Move.*

He started with something basic: wiggling his fingers. He willed them to move, and they obeyed. Carlo next clenched his hands into fists then released them, performing this again and again until the numbness became pins and needles. Eventually, the blood returned to his hands.

Once he was reasonably certain he'd regained enough strength to effectively maneuver his body, he reached for the frame that had once held the windshield and carefully pulled until his body slid forward toward the opening. Feeling was slowly returning to his lower body as well, spreading across his legs and into his feet. But with sensation came further pain as well, a dull ache that pulsed through him from head to toe.

He slumped and fell a bit, his body now twisted and bent nearly in half, but he'd gotten far enough so that his head protruded from the windshield opening. A burst of snowy air slapped his face. Carlo welcomed it, allowing the cold to put a greater distance between consciousness and the darkness that had consumed him earlier. He gasped in the fresh air, filled his lungs with it then coughed it out. His chest stung, and there was an odd burning sensation in his ribs, but he grabbed the frame again and pulled himself completely free of the vehicle.

He slid through and flopped over into the snow facedown, but was able to get to his hands and knees relatively quickly. His neck ached and his head felt heavy as a cinderblock, so he let it hang, his chin nearly touching his chest as he heaved in another series of deep breaths.

Blood plopped in fat drops to the ground, staining the snow as the horrible sound of the crash—that terribly *final* sound of impact— echoed in his ears.

Without lifting his head, his eyes panned the area and located the windshield a few feet from the overturned SUV, shattered and spider-webbed but still whole. He could only hope his head hadn't done all that damage to the glass, but it certainly felt like it had. Pain surged through his skull and fanned down his neck and shoulder blades, joining the array of aches already present in the rest of his body.

Carlo wiped more blood from his eyes then raised his head and attempted a look around. Though still on hands and knees, he was able to make out most of the road up ahead. He stared through the heavy snow until more of the horizon came into focus, and saw the cottages—just snow-draped lumps now—in the distance. He was so close, so close to Katherine.

But then movement from the corner of his eye captured his attention, a subtle movement from above and slightly to his right.

Carlo forced himself up onto his knees and reluctantly lifted his gaze to the snow-draped trees. His vision was still far from perfect, and the heavy snowfall made visibility even worse, but he knew what he was seeing. He blinked rapidly, grappled with what his mind told him could not be, and yet, there it was.

A series of small bodies bound in winter coats, the hoods pulled up over their heads to conceal their faces, sat perched in the trees. Twenty or more were scattered throughout the trees between his position and the lake, and though he could not see their eyes, Carlo knew from the angle of their heads that they were watching him through the snowfall.

He struggled to his feet, knees weak and trembling, eyes wide and mouth agape.

One after the next, the sentinels began to slowly drop from the trees.

Carlo tried to speak, but the words stuck in his throat, any sound muffled by the wind.

Once the small beings had all reached the ground, they moved toward him through the storm in a silent, methodical, and eerily uniform shuffle, arms dangling lifelessly at their sides and bodies perfectly still.

In the distance, something dark broke through the white landscape. Waiting and watching in the road was a person in a knit hat and a long dark overcoat. Though he was too far away for Carlo to make out any facial features, he could tell it was a man.

Just like the lake itself, there is the surface, and there is what lies beneath.

The man advanced toward him with the same otherworldly gait the children possessed, pushing through the deep snow with what appeared to be great effort but progressing nonetheless. In time, unlike the children, Carlo was able to see the man's face. He had the blackest eyes he'd ever seen, and when he looked into them—even at a distance—he was met with a sense of emptiness and sorrow greater than any he had ever before experience. Every moment of sadness, uncertainty, regret, guilt, shame and fear he'd endured in the course of his life soldiered through him to produce a crushing feeling of utter hopelessness and despair. And yet, even with his mind collapsing, Carlo found himself incapable of looking away.

The children continued to shuffle forward, and the man, still just behind them, extended his arms like a great giant bat, his dark overcoat and black eyes beacons in the whiteout.

By the time Carlo was able to process what he was witnessing, he realized the things playing out before him were neither tricks of the storm nor delusions caused by his injuries. Impossible as he knew it to be, the man was really standing there, a victim of crucifixion nailed to an invisible cross, arms out and head bowed.

As the children continued forward, moving closer, the man's

head suddenly snapped back to again reveal his face.

It had changed.

A scream fought its way to the forefront, through the howling wind and endless mass of snowflakes, a scream remarkably pure in its primordial timbre. A scream of terror absolute, the depth and scope of which human beings were rarely able to produce.

But it wasn't until the brood of children closed around Carlo, growling like a pack of wild dogs, tiny hands tugging at him and pulling him back down into the snow, that he realized the scream was his own.

CHAPTER NINETEEN

Katherine did not remember sinking, falling beneath the water and spiraling downward into the murky depths of the lake. She only remembered floating, her arms out and slightly above her head, legs dangling lifelessly below her and her hair hovering and gliding about like a dark aura. The water was chilly and sobering, but not freezing. It stung her eyes, yet she kept them open and fixated on the dull light in the distance overhead, fearful that if she lost sight of it she would never again find her way to the surface. Her bare toes brushed the bottom as the remote sunlight, filtered by the water and plant life surrounding her, cast the lake in a strange emerald tint.

It's all right to sleep now.

Her husband's voice was as clear as if he were floating right next to her.

We all sleep, Katherine.

The need to breathe taunted her, and though the inherent inclination to panic was present, she somehow remained calm.

Even angels in Heaven and demons in Hell sleep.

His voice was echoing now, less natural, but he was still nowhere in sight. Rather than look for him, Katherine continued to stare at light breaking the surface overhead.

Sometimes the Devil himself sleeps.

It looked so very far away.

Even God sleeps, did you know that?

Katherine felt tightness in her chest...

That's when we need to be afraid, my love, when God sleeps.

...a crushing pressure that fanned out across her breasts and up into her shoulders...

Because that's when the Devil opens his eyes and comes awake.

...weighting her down and keeping her suspended there near

the bottom of the lake.

And that's when he makes us remember, Katherine.

She wondered how she was still able to hold her breath.

That's when he makes us see everything we want and need so desperately to forget.

Years of smoking had rendered that capacity virtually impossible for anything other than a few seconds at a clip, and yet…

Those things we wish we could forgive ourselves for…but never do.

Her lungs began to burn and ache, and a spasm rolled through her abdomen.

Because the Devil isn't in the forgiveness business, Katherine.

"James!" she screamed, voice muffled by the water. An explosion of bubbles and air rushed from her mouth and nostrils. See watched it race toward the surface in an oddly beautiful and graceful rush, reminding her once again just how deep the lake was.

But Katherine did not drown.

It's all right to sleep now.

The sunlight changed from an emerald hue cutting through water to a more natural shade. She could feel it now, warming her arms.

The woods…she was in the woods…but not the woods surrounding the lake. This was foreign terrain, a place she had never been before, even in dreams.

A small booklet lay at her feet. She crouched, retrieved it and recognized it as one of the collections of poetry James had published over the years. She opened it to reveal a single poem covering the page facing her.

STEAMING REMNANTS

I will be there soon
I can feel the depth of its power
Not throttling me as I'd once feared
But calling softly, beckoning
As convincing as the color bleeding soundlessly
Through cracked window shades
Revealing a dying sun
And the realities of nature and man.

The noise will stop there

All the rage and mindless violence
Hatred born of ignorance and fear
Slipping away like dew from beveled leaves
And me, falling there
Shattering without pain into endless pieces
Becoming one with all that once made me whole
While absorbing secrets and destinies in silence.

I will be so still and quiet
Not afraid but full of joy
As the last breaths of this world
Flutter off like so many seagulls floating
With both grace and predatory purpose
Above bins filled with steaming remnants
Of what was once alive.

A breeze blew through the trees, and the booklet fell to pieces, disintegrated into ash carried off on the wind.

Katherine followed after it, along a path through the forest, until she emerged into a small clearing. Beyond it, nestled in the forest like the oasis it was, sat a small pond. On the far banks, an old rope hung from one of the larger nearby trees, summoning visions of boys and girls swinging out over the pond then dropping into it, laughing and enjoying a warm summer day much like the one Katherine now found herself in.

But on this day the pond was deserted.

A large boulder sat perched at the edge of the left-hand bank. James sat atop it; his legs pulled up close to his chest, arms wrapped around them and chin resting on his knees. He hadn't seemed to notice her, but Katherine could tell he knew she was there. Nude, as she was, he looked cold despite the warmth from the sun beating down on them, and was still wet from a recent swim. "I never told you about Parker."

Katherine moved closer. "No."

"He was just a boy," he said softly. "But then, so was I."

She noticed the sun through the trees, how it filtered through the foliage and decorated a section of forest just behind James in an intricate pattern of shadow and light. It felt so peaceful here, so safe and serene, a haven for daydreams and flights of childhood fantasy, a place of innocence and joy. And yet, there was something else, horrible and deadly, slithering just beneath this tranquil shell, something that didn't belong. An intruder, a destroyer amidst the beauty, it was wrapped and hidden within it, waiting patiently.

"Most people have no idea what it's like to be alone," James said, "really, truly, utterly *alone*. They think they do, but they don't."

"James, where are we?"

"It's not so bad when you can pick and choose the circumstances, when you can isolate yourself if you want or need to, when you can control it. It's not so bad if you know you have love, are loved, and have that as a sanctuary at your worst points. But when it's decided for you, when it's the hand you're dealt, so to speak, and you have no real love to save you, when you're just a child it..." For the first time, James raised his chin from his knees and looked over at Katherine. "Alone and unloved is something a child should never feel."

"It's something no one should ever feel." Katherine held his gaze.

"Yes, but especially a child," he said.

"I know you had a difficult childhood, James."

"Do you now?" He turned back to the pond before them.

"Yes, and I'm sorry. I'm sorry you had to go through—"

"I thought when I went to live with the Covingtons I'd found something I'd never had before," James said quickly, his voice louder now. "A real family where people cared about one another, where I didn't have to feel so alone anymore...a family, a real, loving family like everyone else. I actually believed it for a while, the way children sometimes believe in things they shouldn't, in things they know aren't true but choose to believe anyway. Because when you're a child you think that maybe—just maybe—if you believe long enough and hard enough, that wishing will make it so. But that's just another lie, like life itself, and when we get older we realize that all the little fibs we tell ourselves from the time we're old enough to comprehend and imagine them only exist so we can make it through."

"Where are we, James?"

"I had a foster brother when I first lived with the Covingtons, a little brother named Parker. He was a beautiful little boy with the brightest eyes I'd ever seen before or since. I still see those eyes every time I close my own. I tried to forget them over the years, and now and then I did. But they always come back. Always, Katherine. Always."

"What happened here?" she asked. "Did something happen here when you were a child?"

"They tell you such lies." Pain dominated his expression. "They tell you they love you the same as they love their own child, and you believe them because you need to so desperately. But it's not true. It's not true because their real child can do no wrong and you can do no right. You're always second best, always coming up short. And it hurts but you accept it because it's all there is. You try so hard to please them, to do your best, but it always falls just shy. And then something happens…something bad…and nothing is ever the same again."

Katherine slowly closed the gap between them until she could reach out and touch his leg. His skin was warm, alive. "What happened here?" she asked again. "What was the bad thing that happened?"

"That bitch Josephine," he said, turning his head so he could rest his cheek against the tops of his knees. "She always blamed me, always accused me. I could never get her to believe me. I didn't hurt Parker. I would never have hurt him, I—he was my little brother."

"Tell me what happened, James."

"The Devil came awake while God slept. In me, he came awake in me."

Katherine reached out in an attempt to hug and console him, but he was sitting up too high on the boulder. With one hand still resting on his thigh, she started up the side of the rock so she could sit with him.

Until she saw what was floating in the pond just beyond the shore.

A young boy floating faceup just beneath the clear water, eyes open but seeing nothing. Eyes long dead.

Katherine staggered back and nearly fell. "I know him," she gasped. "I-I've seen him before, he was on the lake with you when you were crossing the ice with those children. He's the little boy in the gray suit."

James nodded without raising his head. "I didn't kill him, Katherine. I never touched him. I loved him. Josephine always believed I drowned him, she blamed me but I—I didn't do it. I didn't *do* anything."

"How did he drown, James? Tell me how he drowned."

"There used to be a small wooden raft in the middle of the pond," he said dully. "Children weren't supposed to swim here unattended but everyone in town did. Kids were the only ones that came here. I took Parker a lot that summer, and nothing ever happened...until one late afternoon. Parker insisted on swimming out to the raft and back. I wouldn't allow it because I knew he couldn't make it. He'd only just learned to swim with any kind of ability the year before. But I was showing off, swimming out there and back, and he wanted to do it too. I didn't realize how much he looked up to me, how much he loved me too."

Katherine felt her legs tremble, and she slowly sank into a sitting position on the ground. She'd become suddenly lightheaded.

"Parker disobeyed me and started swimming out to the raft. I knew he could make it there all right, so I stayed here on this rock and watched him. I was mad at him for going out there, I wanted to go home, it was late in the day and everyone else had left. I was angry so I stayed here and glared at him. He made it to the raft, climbed up and waved. He was laughing." His face twitched into a smile, but the dark memories wouldn't allow him to sustain it. "I called to him to wait there a few minutes before swimming back so he could catch his breath, but he insisted he could make it and wanted to prove it to me. He was so sure he could do it like a big boy, like—like me. He was wrong."

Katherine felt her eyes fill with tears. How could her husband have carried this with him his entire life and not told her? So much of his inner turmoil and pain now made sense. "You couldn't reach him in time?" she asked.

"He hadn't even gotten halfway back when he started having trouble. I knew he was drowning. He started flailing his arms frantically over his head, and he screamed a few times, trying to call me, but the water was choking him and he couldn't stay afloat."

"James, did you try to—"

"I was just a little boy myself!" he said, anger rising in his voice as he turned his face away from her so she could no longer see him. "I froze, I—I just sat here while he fought to live. And, my God, how that little boy fought. I knew I should've gone into the water for him but I couldn't move. Every fiber in my being was screeching at me, ordering me out there to save that little boy, but I couldn't move. I *couldn't* move. I just sat here, quietly and casually, and watched him drown."

"My God," she whispered, the words escaping her before she could stop them.

"You know nothing of gods," he muttered. "Nothing…and everything."

"I don't understand."

When James turned back to her, his face was streaked with tears. "I ran home and told Josephine and Darren what happened. When we got back he was floating dead in the pond. I knew he'd already be dead. Do you know how I knew that, Katherine? Because he was dead before I left."

"You were just a child yourself," she told him. "You froze, you were frightened, and you froze. It happens to people all the time. It wasn't your fault, do you understand? It wasn't your fault that Parker drowned."

"I should've saved him. I *could've* saved him."

"No, you were in shock and—"

"I *could* have saved him, Katherine," James said, forcefully this time. "But I didn't. I sat here and watched him die instead."

"James, listen to me. You were in shock, you—"

"I didn't kill Parker," he said, an eerie calm returning to his tone. "I didn't do anything. I didn't even try. And somehow, that's worse. It's even more insidious than if I'd drowned him myself. It had to be dealt with, painful as it was and as much as I tried to hide from it. I'm an artist, it's what I do, Katherine. It's who I am."

"You were just a frightened little boy."

"The Covingtons never forgave me," he said as if he hadn't heard her. "Especially Josephine, she always accused me of hurting her precious Parker but never once thought about me and how I felt, what I had gone through. She was horrible to me after that, and Darren, spineless bastard, went along. He hated me too. They never seemed to realize—or maybe they did—that right or wrong, we're all defined in many ways by who we love, and by who loves us. They…"

Katherine wiped tears from her eyes and struggled to hold herself together. "What did they do, James? What did they do to you?"

He slowly slid off the boulder to the ground and knelt at the banks of the pond where Parker's small body was still floating lifelessly. "They stopped lying."

Katherine's fight to control her emotions was a losing battle, as visions of the delicate child James had once been—a damaged and terrified little boy ravaged with guilt and deeply traumatized by what had happened—refused to leave her. Her heart tore in two for that little boy, that sad and frightened and broken little boy.

"They stopped lying to me because they didn't care anymore now that their real child was dead," he said. "But they didn't understand how much I needed those lies. They were all I had. Without them, I had to see the truth. I was alone again, unloved again."

"Until you met me," she said.

"Yes," he sobbed, "until I met you."

"And the Japanese boy?" she asked a moment later. "He was another little boy you couldn't save, and it brought it all back, didn't it?"

"That's when I first knew what was truly happening," he said, continuing to cry. "I knew then it wasn't about Parker or that little Japanese boy. It was about me."

"It made you feel like you'd failed by not somehow being able to save him, and by not saving him it was like not being able to save Parker all over again, wasn't it?" Katherine pressed.

"Don't you understand even now?" he asked, wiping the tears from his eyes and face. "I was *able* to save Parker. I can do whatever the fucking hell I want to do, can't you see that? I chose not to."

"It wasn't a choice," she told him.

"Yes, my love," James said as he slowly rose to his feet, "it was."

"This isn't reality," she said helplessly.

"Reality is perception...and perspective."

Something moved behind him...slowly, sneakily.

An enormous gray snake with black markings slithered over the top of the boulder, down over the side and onto the ground, where it slowly coiled next to him and came to rest. James crouched and ran a hand over the creature's head. It did not seem to mind.

Katherine felt a shiver slowly course through her. She drew her feet closer to her body in an attempt to shrink farther away from the animal. Over the years James had come to know and understand her fear of snakes, and he'd always made an attempt to keep the lake area as clear of them as possible. Whenever one ventured down from the forest he would return it with his usual loving care, aware of how frightened Katherine was of them.

"Cliché, I know, forgive me. But snakes are such wonderfully effective metaphors for evil, don't you think? Unless you're a snake, of course, because from their perspective it's probably demonizing them unfairly in most cases, they're just animals like any other. You see? Perception, my love, it's all perception and perspective."

"You know snakes terrify me," she said softly, as if it might hear.

"Yes, I do." James grinned at her, but there was nothing warm or funny about it. "Fear of snakes is primeval in many people, and why shouldn't it be? The stories of snakes as living embodiments of evil are older than Man. Remember the Garden of Eden? The snake was even there at the dawn of humanity, if you believe in such things. Regardless, it's one of the most misunderstood stories ever. So few people seem to realize that the story isn't about beginnings at all, it's about an end. It's true that something was born in that garden, but something also died there. Man, as God had originally intended, Katherine. All thanks to our little friend here." He ran his fingers across the serpent's body. "And what was left? Mankind scrambling for answers and creating so many religions, so many philosophies to choose from, most with just enough truth and common sense to comfort and control, but none with definitive answers. No, we mustn't have answers from either side, Katherine, because then there would be no need for faith, no need for hatred or love, greed or charity, war or peace, cruelty or kindness. Not in the light, not in the dark."

"What's happening, James, what—"

"Do you know what the Hindus believe?" he asked suddenly.

Katherine remembered the weeks before his disappearance, when he'd become consumed with reading everything he could get his hands on regarding the nature of reality and existence, parapsychology, various religions, philosophy, and strange psychic phenomenon.

"Their gods and demons experience birth and death just as we do," he answered before she could. "They live what seem to be nearly wholly human lives, experiencing the same things we do. Yet they're eternal, because they're not human, Katherine. They're something else, something similar disguised as human. All religions have some truth. That's theirs. That's the part they got right, and I'm living proof. What I never realized was that we always assume gods and demons know what they are, but maybe some are just as lost as humans are here, dumped and expected to wing it, to fight their way through like everyone else. Maybe, just as humans do, they—I—have to search for my true self and nature, and if they're lucky, one day they find it. They find the truth about who and what they are."

I'm not who you thought I was, and I'm not what you thought I was.

"Maybe sometimes," he added, "no matter how hard they try to hide from it...the truth finds them."

I'm not even who I thought I was.

"You're not a god or a demon, James," she said, voice shaking. "You're just a frightened and wounded little boy."

"Can a frightened and wounded little boy do this?" he asked, turning a palm to the sky and sweeping his arm slowly between them to indicate their surroundings. "Can a frightened and wounded little girl like you?"

I can do things human beings cannot do. Things you could never understand even if I was able to explain them to you. What does that tell you?

"And if we live," James said, "then we dream, Katherine. All of us, we dream."

Tell me, Katherine, what do you suppose demons dream?

"Who are the children?" Katherine asked. "Who is the man with them?"

As James lifted the snake onto his shoulder and allowed it to slowly wrap itself around him, the sunlight faded, blurred, and the pond and woods reverted to the depths of the lake from which Katherine had come.

She was beneath the water again, watching the sunlight beyond the surface above.

And then she heard his answer. "The children are mine," his voice whispered to her. "The man is me...and you are my dream."

CHAPTER TWENTY

Whirling like a dervish and punching wildly at the air, Carlo staggered through the deep snow in an attempt to free himself from the children. But as he spun away, tripped and fell into the road, he realized they were gone. He struggled to his feet, and with a quick pivot, frantically searched the trees.

The man in the dark overcoat was gone as well, leaving behind only the cold and gusting wind to fill a landscape both beautiful and deadly. Snow continued to fall, the flakes delicate and tiny now as cloud bursts of Carlo's breath escaped him one after the next.

Night was coming. Fast. Within moments there would be no light but the moon.

Carlo brought his hands to his head, ran them through his wet hair. He was freezing, his head and body ached and he couldn't seem to catch his breath. The terror refused to release him, and instead burrowed deeper. "What's happening to me?" he asked the sky, voice raspy and weak. When it gave no answer, he pushed on toward the main house, toward Katherine, his legs somehow still carrying him as his splintered mind struggled to hold itself together.

I'm going to make it, he told himself. *Keep moving, almost there.*

Amidst the madness, the one thing that had always comforted and protected him emerged and took hold in the forefront of his mind. Humor had always gotten him through, and now his mind raced in an attempt to locate one of the jokes he'd heard over the years—any joke—but he couldn't seem to remember any. *I'm Carlo Damone*, he thought. *I'm the life of the fucking party.* Like whistling past a graveyard, Carlo forced himself to follow that train of thought, knowing it would eventually lead somewhere and help center him. "Guy walks into a bar," he said suddenly, breathlessly, "with a—with a parrot on his head. Bartender says, 'Can I help you?'" He stumbled in the snow and nearly fell before catching his balance.

"Parrot says, 'Yeah, get this guy off my ass.'"

Carlo laughed, telling himself it was funny, the funniest goddamn thing he'd ever heard. His laughter, empty and dull, echoed through the night then vanished, swallowed by the howling winds and replaced instead with a quiet, pained whimper.

Because it wasn't until he'd made his way over an embankment leading to the house that he saw the body in the snow. And this time, it was no nightmarish hallucination.

Lying faceup in the snow between the cabins and the main house, only the upper portion of the body was visible. It faced the house, which was clearly its destination, but had fallen a few dozen yards short of the steps leading to the sliders. From the initial appearance, it seemed like the person had been running through the deep snow, run out of steam, collapsed to its knees then fallen backward, where it had remained until it froze. Draped in a thick sheen of ice and snow, one arm was at its side and partially buried in the snow. The other was extended out in front of and above it, fingers reaching toward the sky as if trying to touch something just beyond their grasp, or perhaps in an attempt to ward something off.

Carlo recognized the painted fingernails, the gaudy jewelry and the fashions only one person would wear in such weather, and as he did so, his knees gave out and he sank into the snow next to her. He harbored hope that perhaps there was some chance he'd reached her time, but it was transitory. Marcy was gone, eyes open and still filled with the terror she'd been experiencing when she'd died, mouth still wide like a gaping wound, forever frozen in mid-scream.

"Motherfucker," Carlo growled with what little strength he still possessed. "She never hurt anyone, why would you—*how* could you do this to her?"

Because loss—death—is a part of life. Isn't that what we're taught to believe?

He scrambled to his feet and staggered about drunkenly, searching the growing darkness for the voice he was certain had just whispered in his ear. But he was alone in the snow now, alone with what remained of Marcy.

In the distance was her SUV, crashed. Anyone coming here would see this scene and quickly determine that she had been the one to crash it and had then attempted to make it to Katherine's house in the blizzard, only to fall short and freeze to death in the snow just feet from the steps. A tragic series of events to be sure, Carlo thought, but nothing unexplainable. "You've got it all figured out, don't you, James? Like one of your fucking stories or poems, it's all plotted out, isn't it?" A gust of wind hit him and nearly knocked him back into the snow. "We'll see, you fucker. If you touched one hair on Katherine's head, I swear to God I'm gonna kill you." Though he couldn't see him, Carlo knew James was there. "You hear me?" he screamed into the night. "I'm gonna fucking kill you with my bare hands!"

Carlo steadied himself, turned away from the wind and looked at the house.

Like the cabins, the main house was dark, but he knew Katherine was somewhere inside, and that he'd find her there. He also knew she wouldn't be alone when he did. Steeling himself, Carlo trudged forward through the snow, calling Katherine's name again and again as he made his way toward the steps.

Katherine felt herself rising, moving slowly but steadily up through the water and toward the surface, toward the light. As her body ascended, in the darker waters below and to her sides, she saw numerous small forms floating along with her. But these other beings were not seeking the surface as she was. Instead, they remained motionless, their small bodies bobbing lethargically, vacant eyes watching her with indifference through the increasingly murky water.

She was within a few feet of the surface when her chest constricted and she again became cognizant of not being able to breathe. Panic set in, but she was almost there. Moving in what felt like slow motion, Katherine reached for the surface with both hands and kicked her feet. The light became brighter, and the water above her began to ripple, disturbed by her impending arrival.

As Katherine broke through the surface she gulped in a deep swallow of air and coughed it back out. Treading water, her hair soaked and matted against her face, dripping into her eyes, she turned slowly in the water in search of the shore.

Until something like small hands closed around her ankles and yanked her back down with a single violent tug.

Katherine.

She opened her eyes. She was back in the house, facing the sliders and sitting on the floor with the shotgun in her lap. The same as she'd been before. Barney lay sound asleep in the chair, and Katherine could hear the strange dripping sound again, and smell the peculiar odor she had prior. Snow had accumulated halfway up the sliders and continued to pelt it with tiny crystals that made an eerie ticking sound against the glass. Like little fingernails tapping it, she thought. Beyond it she could see nothing but the night and more blowing snow.

The dripping sound continued, louder now.

In the distance, or perhaps only in the deep recesses of her mind, she swore she heard a faraway voice calling her name.

Katherine tightened her grip on the shotgun. She could not be sure, but she thought the sound and smell was coming from behind her. The voice she could not pinpoint.

Until a blurry dark mass crashed against the sliders with a resounding thud, pounding against the glass with deadly purpose.

Startled to terror, Katherine screamed, leveled the shotgun and fired.

With a deafening boom, the intruder was blown back and away, airborne and off the steps into the night, wrapped in a shower of shattered glass, blood, and spitting snow.

Carlo wasn't sure exactly what had happened. All he knew was that he was on his back and his abdomen felt like it had been hit by a midsize car. Pain spiked across his chest and across his groin, and a sticky bile and coppery taste coated the back of his throat and inside of his mouth. His first impulse was to scream and writhe about, to move and get to his feet if he could, to inspect himself and to see how badly he'd been injured. But none of that seemed quite possible now. His mind and heart were racing, but his body remained still and quiet; the only things moving within it beyond his control or influence, acting instead on their own and without regard for his condition.

The sky above was dark and hard to see through the ocean of snowflakes, but he thought for a moment he had seen the moon.

He tried to breathe, but with each new breath there came more sharp pain and a gurgling, bubbling surge of blood that exploded up from somewhere deep within him. It burst from his mouth and spattered his chin and face with crimson, and Carlo wondered if perhaps he had died, drowned in his own blood.

But he could still feel the snowflakes peppering his face. They felt good, cooling and comforting somehow.

Carlo tried to speak but only managed to vomit more blood and bile.

And then through the darkness came the faces. The faces of children...or something like children, creations close but not quite exact, not quite perfect. They hovered around and above him, peering down at him with curiosity and a look of near delight.

This is a nightmare, Carlo thought. *It's all a nightmare.*

He remembered the dream from the night before, he could see it all playing out before his eyes like a movie projected on an enormous screen, and realized this wasn't all a nightmare, but *the* nightmare.

And just as in the dream, he heard James laughing somewhere in the night.

Despite what you might think, I always liked you, Carlo. I wish there was another way, some different ending, but there isn't.

"Wake up," he gasped, choking. "Please, I—I want to wake up now."

Don't we all?

Though he could no longer feel much of his body, Carlo suddenly sensed motion.

The memories of the dream dissipated, and he again saw the faces staring down at him. He struggled to see beyond them and up into the dark, snow-filled sky above instead.

It was moving, passing over him.

They're dragging me, he thought. *Christ, they're dragging me through the snow.*

In limited moonlight, and through the swirl of snowflakes, the children soundlessly and slowly towed Carlo back through the deep snow until they had reached the frozen surface of the lake.

On the way he lost consciousness twice, and thought he'd died both times.

When he felt the ice cracking and opening around him like the ragged jaws of some ravenous predator, Carlo realized he hadn't been that lucky.

One by one, the children slipped under the ice and vanished into the lake beneath him, then reached back up with their tiny hands and pulled him under the surface along with them.

Carlo felt a rush of freezing water wash over him, and with a final attempt to scream, felt his abdomen and chest compress as he choked on another explosion of blood.

With arms out at his sides, head back and mouth still bloody and frozen in anger and agony, Carlo's body spun slowly, gracefully turning along the opening until it was pulled from sight and beneath the ice.

From a distance it looked as if the lake had come alive and devoured him.

And it had.

CHAPTER TWENTY ONE

There was no question she'd fired the weapon.

There was also no question she'd hit something.

Ghosts don't bleed.

Still, she could not be certain exactly what she'd shot just seconds before, yet something deep within her suggested it was better that way. Better to not know, it told her, better to let the darkness have its mysteries on this cold, lonely, snowy night.

The blast still rang in her ears, and Barney had bolted from the room at a speed Katherine hadn't known he possessed until that moment. She'd felt the gun kick, lunge back into her chest like she'd been shoved by someone much larger and stronger than she was, and her body still ached from the impact.

Katherine didn't remember dropping the shotgun, but apparently she had, as when she looked down she saw it a few feet from her on the floor. It was still smoking.

What remained of the sliders did little to shield her from the storm beyond. Snow spit through the opening the blast had made, as only the lower portion of the glass remained intact, and that too was badly cracked. Blood, snow and glass lay scattered about the floor, and beyond it, the night watched her silently through the falling snow. So deceptively beautiful, she thought, another lie in the endless string that was her life.

The dripping sound and odd smell returned.

"Stay away from the window for a moment," James whispered from somewhere behind her, lake water slurring his speech as it spewed from his lungs and gurgled past his lips. "They can see us."

"Stop this, James," she said, her voice exhausted and drawn. "Please stop this."

"Do you think any of this is easy for me?"

"I don't know. Is it?"

"It's not all a lie, Katherine," he slurred. "The love is real. *My* love...is real."

"This isn't love, James."

"But it is. It's a greater love that sometimes leaves us no choice but to abandon even those things we love."

Ah, the artist and his demons. Hardly original, my love, but often accurate, the concept of the artist confronted with his or her own artistic manifestations.

"It's the nature of the beast," he told her, "my nature."

"Characters in some demented play, is that all we are to you?" she asked. "Is that all I am to you?"

Rather than answer, a piece of paper blown in with the wind floated across the room and landed within Katherine's reach. With shaking hands, she retrieved it. It was a page torn from one of James's poetry collections on which a single poem had been written.

SKELETAL REMAINS

Deceived by hungry, ravenous compulsion
Distracted by the maddening pitter-patter
Of raindrops tickling awnings on an unseen roof.

Summoned to thunderstorms
Rolling to boiling points beneath skin
Like delicate crystal
Concealed in costumes of arrogance and haste
My armor a futile disguise
Useless
As all I know to be unclean
Beckons, strips me to the bone.

There is nothing beyond the fog
But for illusions in the mind's eye
Cheap parlor tricks
Performed on an ancient dusty stage
By demons grinning with deceit
My pallid skeletal remains just out of reach
As footlights flicker and burst, showering my soul
With sparks and the putrid sweet stench of charred flesh
Signaling the beginning of a new torment
And the end of one

Not yet ripe.

"Words," she said, crumpling the paper and tossing it aside with what little strength she still had. "Empty words."

"Truth, Katherine. Those words are truth."

"It's all perception and perspective, remember?"

"You're angry because you thought I left you," he said through what sounded like a rush of water spilling from his mouth. "Anger is a part of loss, and loss is a part of love. It's the price we pay for it. Even children know there are consequences to love, Katherine."

"Even your children, James?"

"My children even more than others."

"Is it the lake?" she asked hopelessly.

"The lake is only metaphor, my love. Like the snake, it exists as a vehicle, a tool, but as I tried to explain to you once before not so long ago, people are haunted, not places and things."

"Why should I believe you now when so much of everything else has been a lie?"

"Because I'm telling you the truth," he gurgled, "and my truth is the only truth you can ever know."

"And the others?" she asked.

"The same."

She realized then that she could hear him—actually hear him—the sound of his voice was not in her head.

Katherine closed her eyes, remembered swimming in the lake. Not with James, but alone, on a cool summer night. The moon had been more full and luminous than normal that night, providing an unusual amount of light. She remembered moving, gliding through the water, swimming from one end of the lake to the other and then back again, feeling alive and refreshed and happy. Hadn't she felt happy?

Yes, my love. Very happy is how I remember it too.

She remembered reaching the dock and pulling herself up, and how the water fell free of her, trickling away in steady streams. As she held tight to the edge of the dock, an enormous moon hung in the otherwise dark sky behind her, so perfect it looked as if it had been painted there.

In the not so far distance she saw the house. The tourist season would begin in less than a week, but for now, the cabins remained dark and vacant. In the house James had left a few lights on, and she could see him sitting in an easy chair with a book in his lap. Across the back of the chair sat Barney, gazing down at him lovingly.

Katherine let go, pushed away from the dock and slowly sank beneath the surface.

She tried to remember what had filled her dreams that night, but couldn't.

Perhaps it was better not to remember. Perhaps it was better instead to remember that sometimes there was hope in places one never expected to find it. Sometimes there was even hope in the uncertainty of a still summer night, in the howling winds of a winter blizzard, or even in the psychotic darkness of another's nightmare.

Because there is beauty even in the darkest art.

Katherine...

She opened her eyes and looked to what remained of the sliders and those gathered on the other side, staring at her with dead poetic eyes, chapped mouths opening and closing like hungry baby birds, small fingers scratching the already broken glass.

Children of the lake, all. James's children.

She would see them in more than just dreams now.

Katherine would've screamed, had she thought it might make a difference. But it no longer mattered, no one could hear. In the morning they would all be gone—she along with them—and amidst the buildings, snowdrifts and deserted cabins, only the lake, and madness unseen would remain.

ABOUT THE AUTHOR

The son of teachers, Greg F. Gifune was educated in Boston and has lived in various places, including New York City and Peru. A trained actor and broadcaster, earlier in his life he appeared in various stage productions and worked in radio and television as an on-air talent, writer and producer, and also held a wide range of jobs encompassing everything from journalism to promotions. Often described as "one of the best writers of his generation" (Roswell Literary Review) and "Among the finest dark suspense writers of our time" (author Ed Gorman) Greg is an acclaimed, internationally published author who has penned several novels and novellas as well as two short story collections. His work has been published all over the world, has been translated into several languages, and has recently garnered interest from Hollywood. His work is consistently praised by critics and readers internationally (including starred reviews in Publishers Weekly, Library Journal, Kirkus, and Midwest Book Review), and his novel The Bleeding Season is considered by many to be a modern classic in the horror genre. Also an accomplished editor, Greg was editor of the popular fiction magazines The Edge: Tales of Suspense and Burning Sky for seven years, where he helped launch the careers of many name writers working in various genres today. Greg was also associate editor at Delirium Books for three years, and for more than a decade has worked as a freelance novel editor for numerous up-and-coming as well as established professionals. He presently serves as editor at Darkfuse Publications. Greg resides in Massachusetts with his wife Carol, their dogs Dozer and Bella, and a bevy of cats. For more information on his work, Greg can be found on Facebook and Twitter.

Curious about other Crossroad Press books?
Stop by our site:
http://store.crossroadpress.com
We offer quality writing
in digital, audio, and print formats.

Enter the code FIRSTBOOK
to get 20% off your first order from our store!
Stop by today!